I0733237

Honeymoon for Four

CHRIS KENISTON

Indie House Publishing

MORE BOOKS
By Chris Keniston

Hart Land
Heather
Lily
Violet
Iris
Hyacinth
Rose
Calytrix
Zinnia
Poppy

Farraday Country
Adam
Brooks
Connor
Declan
Ethan
Finn
Grace
Hannah
Ian
Jamison
Keeping Eileen
Loving Chloe
Morgan

Aloha Series Beach Read Edition:
Aloha Texas
Almost Paradise
Mai Tai Marriage
Dive Into You
Look of Love

Love by Design
Love Walks In
Shell Game
Flirting with Paradise

Honeymoon Series

Honeymoon for One
Honeymoon for Three
Honeymoon for Four

ACKNOWLEDGMENTS

It has been so much fun returning to the Caribbean world of the Honeymoon Series. As soon as we came up with the idea I knew it would be a fun book to write.

As I write more books, I can't imagine bringing new stories to you without the support and encouragement of friends both in and out of the author community. Once again I needed the input of my friend Cheryl Lucas, and this time her mom joined in for the idea-fest! Plotting days with authors Kellie Coates Gilbert, Kathy Ivan, Barb Han and Cindy Dees have become a must in my world. Thank you all!

Now, put your feet up, pour yourself a cool drink, and enjoy a few hours of fun in the sun! I'm hoping you enjoy this sea voyage as much as I did.

CHAPTER ONE

"What you really need is a man."

If Angie Cannon had a nickel for every time her friend Pam had told her that, she could afford to buy all the houses on her block. "I know you and Gil are happy as the proverbial clam, but I prefer solving my problems on my own. A man isn't the answer."

"It could be if you find the right one." If anyone could be considered an expert on that point, it would be Pam. The tall, attractive, and always colorfully dressed redhead had married her first love and first husband for the second time two years ago. In between, she'd gone through three more husbands and one fiancé before finding her happily ever after.

"What I need is a roommate. That would offset the surprise expenses." When her dishwasher had exploded unexpectedly last year in a rather bitter winter freeze, she'd been able to make do washing dishes by hand until she was comfortable springing for the seriously quiet dishwasher she wanted. Waiting for her budget to be happy wasn't an option with her water heater. Cold showers and she would never be friends. "Too bad I don't have a sister. Then I could do like the Ummarinos next door."

Pam shrugged. "You and your mom seem to spend a good deal of time together, especially since your dad passed on. Heaven knows, you guys get along better than any mother and daughter I know."

"It's not hard. Mom has always been my friend too."

"I know. And normally I would never suggest inviting your mother to live with you since it would cramp your style, but in all the years I've known you, the most exciting thing in your style seems to be staying up late with a favorite movie and a bag of real buttered popcorn. At least with your mom you'd have someone to talk to who can talk back."

Angie shook her head. "I offered right after Dad passed. She wouldn't hear of it." Besides, she wasn't about to tell Pam that she and her mother sounded like a broken record when it came to reminding Angie that she needed to get out more, needed to meet people, needed to not work so many hours, needed to stop being married to her job. Though somehow she had always thought moving up the corporate ladder would provide security for her old age. She just hadn't thought how fast the years would go by, or how much more difficult finding the perfect man for her—if there was such a thing—would be with each of those passing years.

The doorbell rang at the same time the knob turned and the heavy wooden front door flung open.

"I spoke to Uncle Tony. He's agreed to give you the family discount. There just might be one small catch." Mina, Angie's next-door neighbor and the oldest of three sisters who had bought her friend Michelle's old house, came to a screeching halt. "Oh, I'm sorry. I shouldn't have barged in."

"I knew you were coming back, it's fine." Angie waved off her neighbor's embarrassment, and gestured toward Pam. "You remember my friend, Pam."

"That's right." Mina extended her hand. "Your husband was the one who helps hang Angie's Christmas lights."

Pam grinned and nodded. "Just one of the things he's good at."

Angie managed to avoid shaking her head, but she couldn't resist a slight eye roll.

On the other hand, Mina seemed to take Pam's innuendo in stride without skipping a beat. "I don't know about anything else, but even my father gave his nod of approval to your husband's work. And trust me, Vito Ummarino does not give praise easily." Mina twisted her wrist in an upward gesture. "Unless, of course, you're

Italian, then you can do no wrong."

"On that note," holding up the massive lobster pot, Pam stepped around Angie and her neighbor, "I had better get home. When I left my husband and his college buddy, they were already holding lobster races. They could all be halfway to Nebraska by now."

"Enjoy." Angie gave her friend a hug and closed the door quietly behind her.

Mina stuck her hand out, holding the sheet of paper. "The nice thing about a really big Italian family is that there's always a relative around who can fix something broken. The downside is even when nothing is broken, there's still always a relative around."

"Thank you. I've been so focused on paying this house off early that I didn't leave enough emergency funds for back to back breakdowns."

"Um." Mina nibbled lightly on the corner of her lower lip. "I should warn you, though."

Angie glanced up from the paper in her hand.

"Uncle Vito is a really good plumber. He considers Angela an Italian name, which in his book already made you like family."

"I sense a *but* coming."

"More of a heads up. My cousin Giovanni is happily single, but my uncle Vito doesn't think there is such a thing. So he might try to do a little… matchmaking."

"How little?"

Mina shrugged. "Could be anything from hoodwinking my cousin the accountant into helping his father install the water heater, to inviting you over for Sunday dinner."

"That doesn't sound too bad." Still, the look on Mina's face made her nervous.

"Do you remember that movie *My Big Fat Greek Wedding*?"

"Doesn't everyone?"

"Well," Mina shrugged again, "that's my family, only we're Italian. If you don't mind them imbedded in your life from time to time, and can ignore the fact that half the famiglia is named either Anthony, Tony, Antonio or

Antoinette, it's not so bad. But the discount should be worth it."

"Sounds like a plan. Thanks again."

"Any time. And if you don't have any plans later, my mom's dropping off a baked ziti. Apparently she doesn't think that she taught the three of us how to cook, and it's always enough food to feed a Marine battalion. We don't mind sharing the calories."

Angie chuckled. She doubted the three sisters had any idea what homemade Italian cooking did to the waistline of a woman over thirty. On the other hand, depending on the outcome from uncle Vito and cousin Giovanni, a little comfort food by dinnertime might come in handy. "I'll let you know."

With a wave, Mina was out the door and darting across the lawn, and Angie's phone was sounding off the ringtone assigned to her mother. "Hi Mom."

"Hey sweetie. How's your day going?"

"Water heater gave up the ghost."

"Oh, honey. At least you're done."

"Done?"

"They say everything comes in threes. Your dishwasher, your spare tire, and now the water heater. You're done. The rest of the year should be easy."

Her mom had to remind her that after finding her tire flat as a pancake the other morning, she soon discovered the spare was no help. Both tires had to be replaced. Hopefully her mother was right, because Pam could do with a worry-free rest of the year. "What's cooking on your end?"

"Well," her mom's tone perked up, "I decided to make a change."

Angie wasn't all too sure she liked the sound of that. "Really? What kind of change?"

"I'm taking a vacation."

Relief whooshed through her. For as long as Angie could remember, Julia Cannon was a sweet and warmhearted woman to anyone who met her. For Angie, her mom had been her first best friend, her number one cheerleader, and her shoulder to cry on when life didn't seem quite fair. Everything good and fun about life, Angie had learned from her mom. Except, since Angie's dad died, her mom had become a bit of a homebody. The last few weeks, something had been off. Her mother had been less chatty, and a little busier than usual. Not that that was a bad thing. Angie wanted her mom to have a full life, she just couldn't help worrying about her at least a little. Of the few close friends her mom had, only one wasn't married and might be free to travel with her mother. "That's nice. Who are you going with? Mabel from your canasta group?"

"No." The extra beats of silence put the nervous knot back in Angie's stomach. "I'm taking a cruise."

"Alone?"

Her mom cleared her throat. "No."

Now the knots in Angie's stomach were twisting like wet twine as she waited for the rest of the story her mom was slow to spit out.

"I'm getting married."

Another hour at his desk and Devon Miller was convinced he'd be permanently cross-eyed.

"You know, if you had a wife and family, you wouldn't spend so much time working." Standing in the doorway, his dad blew out a soft sigh. "Seriously, it's way past quitting time. You really should call it a day."

As far as Dev was concerned, Raymond Miller had been the perfect father. Despite a high pressure corporate career, he'd attended every sporting event, school performance, done daily homework, participated in all the required father-son after school camping or scouting or who knows what activity, and given Devon all the support he had needed to get through college and his MBA. Both his mom and dad had ensured his childhood memories were damn near idyllic. Unfortunately, Raymond Miller the retiree had become a bit of a nag.

"Nice to see you, Pop." His fingers unfolded from

around the mouse and he closed his laptop. According to the clock on the wall, at nearly seven-thirty it was time to call it a day or he really would be cross-eyed forever. "You're here just in time to cook a good medium rare steak at a respectable enough time to call it dinner."

"Oh, actually I already ate."

Dev did a double take to see if he'd misread the time. His father had always been a late supper guy.

"Let's get out of here and take a walk."

"A walk?" He and his dad shared a lot of things, but an evening walk wasn't one of them. Slowly, he pushed away from the desk and straightened to his full height. His mind made a feeble attempt to process all the possibilities for what had his father looking so serious, and what would require the distraction of a walk to tell Dev about it.

"You really never should play poker." Shaking his head, Raymond Miller led the way down the hall.

"What?" It had been a long day for Dev, but usually following his father's train of thought wasn't so challenging.

"I'm not dying or anything like that." His father paused in the front doorway. "I simply wanted to talk without being interrupted by the dinging or buzzing of technology."

Despite the reassuring health update, nothing in Dev was relaxing. The look on his dad's face made it pretty obvious to any son with eyes that this conversation wasn't going to be about cutting calories and skipping sugar in his coffee. But what?

The front door latched shut behind them and his father waited till they'd left the front yard behind before speaking. "It's been a long while since your mom passed."

Dev nodded. He'd just graduated college when his parents let him know his mother had been dealing with a cancer diagnosis. They'd known it was a losing battle for a while, but hadn't wanted his last year of college, or his grades, tainted by worry for his mom. Even at the time, he'd doubted the extra parties and escapades had been worth missed weekends with his mother, but with time, the guilt had eased, and he'd come to understand that he would have dumped that same guilt on her every weekend if he'd come home instead of enjoying his last year. It had been a no-win situation. At least he'd been blessed with a little more time. Not enough, but more.

"And you know that I've been spending more time at the senior center."

When his dad, who refused to consider himself old, had told Dev he'd started going to the senior center a few months back, Dev suspected then that it might have something to do with looking for female company. A sudden recollection from his teenage years of his dad's serious expression and need to walk as they had talked about growing up in general, and girls in particular, flashed in Dev's memory banks. This was the birds and the bees talk all over, except now it was probably more about his dad than controlling teenage hormones. He'd bet anything his father was looking for someone to keep company with. Or maybe had already found her. Now the whole walking thing made sense to him. His dad had a girlfriend. Though his father could have told him that on the living room sofa.

"The center has lots of things to do. New people to meet."

Doing his best not to grin at his dad's approach, he kept quiet and nodded.

"But not the same as doing things with your mom."

The elation at thinking his dad had found someone new slipped away like a leaky balloon.

"A couple of weeks ago I signed up for one of those online things."

"Things?" Good grief. Was his dad doing online dating?

"You know. Meeting people with the same interests as you."

Yeah, Dev knew. Once upon a time his friend Pete had convinced him he was too young to be working so hard and dating so infrequently, so he let himself be talked into trying one of those dating apps. He'd met a few nice women, no one special, and a few with a screw or two loose. A sense of discomfort crept up his spine. At his father's age, cyberspace was filled with scammers and gold-diggers waiting for a kind old soul like his dad to take advantage of.

"I met someone."

And there it was. Now the question at hand was how to casually vet this new friend without insulting his father. "I'm guessing you like her?"

His father's face brightened as he nodded.

That smile on his dad's face had been a long time coming. Suddenly, Dev realized just how much was at stake, and he prayed this really was a sweet older woman looking for a partner and not a way to siphon his dad's savings.

Without breaking step, his dad cast a sideways grin at his son. "You'd like her too, I think."

"Great." Dev needed to give this gal the benefit of the doubt. Why borrow trouble until there were signs of something amiss. "When do I get to meet her?"

His father's hand wound behind his neck. "Well, that's the problem."

"Problem?" Was that the first sign? This talk with his dad felt like a ride on a rollercoaster, never knowing when the next dip would send his suspicions flying into high gear.

"You see, I'm taking a little vacation."

Dev nodded again, waiting for the next shoe to drop, after all, he doubted his dad planned to take this little vacation alone. Assuming the new woman was real and not a man named Mary in some hard to pronounce foreign country.

"A cruise, actually."

"Cruise?" Interesting choice for a man who claimed not to like the beach.

His dad nodded and reaching the corner, turned around to walk back toward Dev's house. "I'm almost all packed. Flying to Florida tomorrow. The ship sails the next day."

"That's pretty fast." Dev kept his hands in his pockets and his thoughts on the facts. "How long will you be gone?"

"Two weeks." His dad stared ahead. Lips pressed tightly together, he seemed to be struggling with words.

Maybe Dev should give his father a little help. "This new friend going with you?"

His father seemed to lose some of the tension in his shoulders. "Yes, as a matter of fact."

If it was at all possible, this conversation was even more awkward than the one Dev remembered from junior high.

"I know she and I haven't known each other long," his father continued, "but at our age, you can't really waste any time when you've found the right one."

Dev was reaching a point in his life where he understood not wanting to waste time, but something wasn't sitting right. "How long have you known her?"

"Bout two weeks."

"Two weeks?" Dev snapped his mouth shut in an effort to hide his surprise. Even if this person was real, and not a scammer from some godforsaken country, two weeks wasn't long enough for anyone to sail off into the sunset.

"I suppose without these newfangled video calls, we wouldn't have made up our minds so fast." His dad's hand hooked around his neck again. "I mean, heaven knows that plenty of my courting your mother took place over the phone, but this video phone thing is much different."

"It is." What more could Dev say? At least it seemed with a face to a name, he could rule out a man from overseas. And what right did he have to pour cold water on his dad's good mood? What harm would a little trip with a woman do? It wasn't like Dev had never gotten friendly fast with some of the women in his own past.

Back at the front door, his father came to a stop. Straightening his shoulders and lifting his chin, he took in a big deep breath and pulled a black velvet ring box from his pocket. Shaky fingers flipped it open.

The sparkling gem almost blinded Dev. His mother would never have been caught dead in a rock that size. It must have set his father back a pretty penny. "Don't you think that's a little overkill to give a ring like that to a woman you've only known a couple of weeks?

"This woman is special. She deserves the best."

Score one for a gold-digger.

"Besides, this trip is..." Raymond Miller cleared his throat. "Uh...themed."

"You mean like Everything Elvis, or Great Gatsby?"

His father closed the lid and slipped it back into his pocket. "It's a destination wedding cruise."

CHAPTER TWO

"**S**he is out of her ever loving mind." Angie paced in Mina's kitchen and stared down at her cell phone. "Two weeks. Who marries a man they've only known two weeks? And via screen time, no less."

"Well—"

"They've never actually met in person. He could be anybody. A fugitive. An ex-con. A wife beater. Maybe he's one of those human traffickers?"

"Okay." Mina sat her friend down at the kitchen table. "Calm down before you have a heart attack or something."

"Here." Ginny, the middle sister, handed her a glass of red wine. "Take a sip. It'll do your blood pressure good."

There was no taking a sip. The glass made it halfway to Angie's lips when the overwhelming aroma of strong alcohol almost made her teary-eyed. "What is this?"

"Chianti. It's Papa's solution to good health and steady nerves."

"I think I'll pass." Red wines weren't her favorite, but this one seemed strong enough to knock an elephant off his game. She set the glass down beside her and muttered *two weeks* to herself for the umpteenth time since talking to her mother.

"It's the *never met in person* part that worries me more than the two weeks." Jo, the youngest of the three sisters, sat at the table, her laptop open. "Which cruise line is it again?"

"She didn't say. But it sails from Florida day after tomorrow and it's a wedding themed cruise. She actually had the nerve to tell me guests weren't allowed. Some malarkey about too many people."

"Got it!" Jo did a fist pump. "A two week cruise for the wedding package. First seven days are on board as a bachelor and bachelorette send off, and then the next seven are the honeymoon portion with mostly moonlit nights at sea and one stop on the cruise line's private island for a day of frolicking in the sun."

"Frolicking in the sun?" Mina asked.

"Hey," Jo waved her hand in a very broad gesture, "their words, not mine."

"What I don't get is why are you here in our kitchen instead of at your mother's talking some sense into her?" Ginnie seemed to be the most practical of the three siblings.

"Because she isn't home from shopping—yet—I drove by to check before walking over here. Her car was gone and the lights were all out." Angie blew out a slow breath and averted her eyes to hide how embarrassed she felt. She'd made the short fifteen minute drive not once, but twice.

"Could the car have been in the garage?"

Angie shook her head. "A car hasn't fit in that garage since my high school graduation."

"Okay." Ginnie, plopped onto the seat beside her and shoved a dish of cookies at her. "So now what do we do?"

The glass beside her, Angie ran a finger along the rim. "I have to find a way to talk some sense into her."

"Well." Mina raised both her arms in a preacher-like movement. Angie had grown used to all the talking with hands these sisters did. "You've got one night till she boards that plane. Not a lot of time."

"Mina's right." Ginnie nodded. "You need more time."

Jo looked up. "Can you keep her from catching the flight?"

"Probably, but only one flight. There are flights to port cities almost every blasted hour on cruise days."

"Yeah, that won't work." Mina shook her head. "But maybe if you had her undivided attention for the three hour plus flight, perhaps you could talk some sense into her."

"I doubt it." She lifted the wine glass and stared, she'd rather have a mild white wine. Strong drinks and her did not mix well. As much as she both loved and regretted drinking all those deceivingly delicious Heavenly Haze's when they were in Santo Domingo for Pam's wedding and Angie's one and only cruise, she also knew diet cola wasn't going to sooth her frazzled nerves. This was serious. Resisting the urge to hold her nose, she dared a sip of the dark wine. Felt it burn all the way down to her toes and then, smacking her lips, bobbed her head. "Not bad."

Jo laughed. "No. Chianti can be an acquired taste for some. Our father watered it down and added sugar when we were young. But we can all hold our liquor."

Too bad Angie couldn't say the same thing. Already feeling a tad more relaxed, she still had a problem to solve. "I spent over an hour on the phone with her before she insisted she needed to run out for a few more last minute things, and I finally agreed to take her to the airport in the morning. Now she's not answering the phone."

"And not home." Mina looked to her sisters and out the window a second before facing Angie. "Looks to me like the only thing you can do is plan B."

"Plan B?" She didn't even have a plan A.

"How's your credit?" Jo asked.

"My credit?"

Jo nodded. "Not all passengers are part of the destination wedding and honeymoon package. This line cuts off bookings twenty-four hours before sailing. That leaves you nineteen hours to make up your mind and pull out your credit card."

"You want me to take a honeymoon cruise?" Had the girls been sipping the Chianti before she'd stormed in the back door ranting about her crazy mother?

Jo nodded. "That'll give you seven days to size up the groom and convince the bride that this is not a good idea."

"How much is it?" Mina looked over her sister's shoulder. "Oh, that's not too bad."

"If there are rooms left on the ship, last minute bookings can be real bargains."

"And you know this how?" Ginnie narrowed her gaze at her little sister.

Again, hands waved forcefully in the air. "Duh, the

computer age. Do you live under a rock? The concept can't possibly be anything new to you."

"I suppose." Ginnie leaned back in her seat and faced Angie. "She may have a point. If you're willing?"

Following her mother on the cruise was insane. Ludicrous. Not in the budget.

"Yes or no?" Jo asked. "Do we book it?"

"What will I do? How will I stop her?"

"We have faith in you," Mina smiled.

Faith. Angie sighed. Maybe inspiration would strike when she got on the ship. She couldn't do nothing. This might be her only chance to save her mother from some unsavory fate and winding up on one of those late night missing person shows. She'd just have to think of something. "Book it."

"Pop, how much do you really know about this woman?" Dev had gone around in circles with his dad for most of the night.

"Look." Raymond Miller stood as tall as Dev and his dark hair had gone salt and pepper at a young age. A fate Dev had escaped by inheriting his mother's sandy hair. Shaking his head, his father zipped the suitcase and turned to face his son. "It's late. I'm tired. I agreed it made sense for you to sleep here tonight so you wouldn't have to drive over and pick me up at zero-dark-thirty in the morning to catch the first flight of the day. I'm sorry the organizers aren't allowing guests but you'll meet when we return, and as soon as we find a new house, we'll even have you over for dinner—"

"New house?"

"Yes. You don't think I'm going to move her into your mother's house, do you?"

"I guess not."

"I thought something in Highland Park might be nice."

"Highland Park? Pop, that's some of the most expensive

real estate in the county."

"You don't think we deserve to live some place nice?"

This was not going the way he wanted. Hooking his hand around his neck, he sucked in a long breath. "Look, Pop, doesn't it strike you as odd that this woman needs expensive jewelry and houses? This is exactly why rushing is not—"

"Stop. It's late and I'm tired. If you plan to nag me all night long—"

"No, Pop. It's just, marriage seems so…permanent."

"At my age everything seems permanent."

"You're not that old."

"No, and I'm not that young either." Raymond shoved the bag to the side of the night stand. "You know I loved your mother more than life itself."

"I know, Pop."

"This is not in any way a reflection of my feelings for her."

"Of course not." Truth was, Dev had hoped for years now that his father would find someone to keep him company. Just not someone he knew so little about. His dad lived a very low-key life, but a man didn't climb the corporate ladder as high as his father had without creating a more than comfortable portfolio. If someone wanted to go hunting, there would be plenty to take and leave his father high and dry.

"Then it's settled. I could have thirty more years in me or I could have thirty minutes. No sense in wasting time." His father shot him one of those pointed glares from Dev's childhood and he knew there was no point in continuing this discussion. "I'd like to get some sleep now."

Dev nodded and took a step back. "Love you, Pop."

His father's stern stance eased. "I love you too."

The bedroom door shut behind his father, Dev wandered into the kitchen. He wasn't quite ready to go to bed and spend the night tossing and turning. One thing he couldn't fault his father for was failure to stock the fridge. Granted, Raymond Miller wasn't the cook his mother once was, but there was no fear of going hungry. Choosing the sourdough bread that had no doubt been bought at the local Saturday morning farmer's market, Dev loaded the slices with cold cuts and grabbed a beer, then doubled back for a bag of chips. Deciphering this dilemma required plenty of fuel.

Foregoing the kitchen table, he made his way to the den, flopped into his father's broken in recliner, and flipped on the television. The first bite of the sandwich satisfied his rumbling stomach instantly. He really should make time to hit the market himself on Saturday mornings. There was no comparing fresh baked bread to manufactured loaves. It wouldn't kill him to skip a few take outs and cook a meal himself. His mom had taught him more than a thing or two about cooking, promising some day he'd make a woman very happy. Halfway through the sandwich, he grew tired of the World War II movie and settled on a rerun of *The Big Bang Theory*. The lead character Sheldon reminded him of his roommate freshman year of college. Too smart and serious for his own good, and only fifteen years old at the time.

He'd made another sandwich and tore through two more bags of chips, going for a third, before the flyer on the side of the refrigerator caught his eye. How had he missed that? The massive ship sketched in blue and red should have stuck out like a sore thumb on the all white appliance. Pulling the sheet off the fridge, he walked back to the recliner, carefully reading the advertisement. Everything lined up. The sail date. The wedding theme. Bachelor and Bachelorette schedules followed by honeymoon romance. All totaling fourteen days.

He sank into the most comfortable seat in the room again, reading the fine print. There was a lot more to this cruise than his father had mentioned. Daily excursions. Evening parties. Planned get togethers from couple's massages and spa days to dance lessons and cooking classes. Plenty of bonding time before the big day. And hopefully plenty of time to realize what a colossal mistake getting married would be.

Ship to shore calls were no longer the expensive and

complicated thing of just a decade ago. Internet plans covered cell phone usage and a passenger could stay as in touch with the outside world as he or she wanted to. Or, more likely, as out of touch as his father probably preferred. Blast.

Another glance at the now empty fridge and a crazy thought exploded. Could it be? Was it possible? He pulled his phone from his pocket and in only a few swipes his crazy idea was confirmed. A few more strokes and the crazy idea was a done deal. According to the timestamp on his phone this was no time to call his boss, but he knew for a fact the man shut his phone off when he went to bed and didn't turn it on till morning. A few well chosen words and the text was ready to hit send.

Family emergency. Need a couple of weeks off. Catching flight out of town tomorrow night. Will bring work computer and check in.

He was going to have a bunch of really ticked off clients, but on the bright side, there were plenty of associates to cover for him. Competent associates. Even if they weren't, this was his dad's future. His old age. His happiness. The whole idea was a no brainer. At least Dev hoped so. Finger hovering over the screen, he sucked in a deep breath and tapped SEND. He had no idea under the Caribbean sun how he was going to do it, but like it or not, he was going to save his father from himself.

CHAPTER THREE

"How's it going?" The speaker from Angie's cell phone filled the small cabin with Mina's voice. "I boarded a couple of hours ago, but they only let us in the rooms a few minutes ago. I'm unpacking."

"Any sign of your mother and her, uh, friend?"

Clearly Mina had no idea how big this ship was. "Not yet, but I'm hopeful. There's an itinerary on my bed for the ship. Looks like the wedding group have a billboard by the concierge desk."

"Well, that should help."

Closing a drawer, she opened another. "It will. I already know there's a cocktail party in one of the lounges right after we set sail. I'm hoping I can at least spot Mom."

"Have you tried calling her?"

That had almost been the first thing Angie had done, then she decided with seven days ahead of her, she'd rather take a little time to check out the guy her mom was so intent on marrying. "I think I want to get the lay of the land first."

"Good idea. Recognizance. Just like special forces."

Special forces? "I was thinking more like an athletic scout. Seeing who all the players are."

"Yes. Better analogy. Who knows, maybe you'll meet a nice guy while you're getting laid. Of the land that is."

She could hear the chuckle in Mina's voice and if she weren't so on edge about who this man was in her mom's life, she would have laughed too. "I'm almost done here. I didn't buy the phone plan so my connection will evaporate when we're out of US waters, but my phone should work in every port."

"Oh, good. I was afraid I was going to have to wait the

whole two weeks to find out what happens."

"No. As soon as I can, I'll let you know what I learn."

"Well, if you get his name, text it to Jo. She's a whiz with digging around on the internet. If there's any dirt on this guy, she'll find it."

"Will do. I'd better run. I have a few more things to unpack and then I'm going to head to the deck for when we leave port."

"You can do this!"

Disconnecting the call, she sucked in a deep breath, slid the empty suitcase under the bed and glanced out the window. "Hope this guy doesn't think Mom has money or he'll be in for an awfully rude awakening."

"I know. I know." Dev kicked his cabin door shut behind him. Setting everything up for an unplanned absence had taken longer than he'd expected. Instead of leaving last night, he'd caught the only morning flight available and made it to the ship just in time. "It couldn't be helped."

"This isn't like you." Dev's boss had swung back and forth from total understanding to complete misery with the predictability of a metronome. It was starting to get on Dev's nerves. "Twelve years and this is the first time you've just taken off."

"Then I guess I'm due."

"Yes." His boss sighed. No doubt a swing back in the direction of understanding. "You're due. Just do me a favor and don't take all your accumulated vacation days at once or the place may fall apart without you."

He hadn't noticed over the last several years that he'd taken fewer and fewer personal or vacation days to the point that he had an obscene number of paid vacation days wracked up. "I promise. No more than two weeks."

"Make sure to let me know if you need anything."

"Will do." He scanned the ship's itinerary that had been left on his bed and studied the section for the wedding attendees. "Gotta run."

Reading more carefully, he made note to check the update board by the front desk. For the entire flight, he'd gone over in his head how to break it to his father that he was on this ship. No matter what lame excuse he came up with, no matter how he sliced it, everything led to the same conclusion. At best, he was here to spy, at worst, here to break up the wedding. For his father's sake, he just hoped there wouldn't be any reason to haul the bride-to-be off to jail. In the meantime, he finished unpacking and made his way to the main deck. Throngs of people leaned along the railing, laughing, waving, drinking, all waiting for the ship to move. By the pool, a calypso band of some sort played festive music clearly meant to put the passengers in the mood for a fun vacation. Though from what he could see, the music was an unnecessary perk. Everyone looked more than ready to partake in the promised fun in the sun.

By the time the ship blew the required whistles to announce movement, he'd downed a cold beer and surprisingly found his toes tapping to the music. He also wondered how in the heck was he going to find his father and friend among all these people? The music grew louder and he decided now that the ship was moving, a slow stroll around deck and then downstairs to learn more was in order.

At the front desk or whatever it was called, he stopped to read the board for the destination wedding group. His eyes almost popped out of his head when he saw the small note to the side showing over three hundred couples had signed up. Who knew that many people wanted to get married off shore. He might need another beer. Suddenly he was feeling very in over his head. Not that three hundred couples planning to marry was any more daunting than the overall number of passengers on this floating resort hotel, but he was slowly beginning to accept that calling his father might be a necessity. Then he'd hope the man would let him meet the bride.

How did Angie find herself once again on a cruise alone? At least last time, even if she didn't have a date, she had friends. This time she didn't know a soul. Except, of course, for her mother—if she could find her. And that was the next mission. As Mina had said, a little recognizance. The lounge entrance for the destination wedding groups welcome aboard had three sets of double doors at a wide hallway. To her surprise, there were only a few couples in line waiting for the doors to open. Looking at the banner set up by the entry, she read the welcome note and stopped cold at the last words. *Private party for Destiny's Destination Wedding couples only.* She looked at the few couples lingering in line. Not only were they obviously paired off, they were all glued to each other like a pair of static clinging socks pulled from a dryer. "Not what I bargained for," she muttered, taking a step in retreat. "Not what I bargained for at all."

One foot firmly in place behind her, she spun about and slammed hard into a solid wall of man.

"Careful." His fingers curled around each of her arms, helping her stand steady. "What were you saying?"

"Uh." Deep grey eyes filled with their own turmoil peered down at her. "Not what I expected," she mumbled.

Leaving his hands up and ready if she stumbled again, he took a half step back and sighed, his gaze drifting to the sets of double doors. "Me neither."

"She changed her mind?"

His gaze snapped back to her. "She?"

"Your fiancée?"

"Oh." His eyes rolled and he almost laughed. "Heavens no. I'm single, but it's a big ship and I was hoping to… find someone here."

Her head bobbed. "Me too."

The doors opened and smiling people, two at each door, stood tablet in hand, waving the couples inside.

"Looks like I'll have to wait until later." He looked over her head, watching the growing line of people shuttle inside.

"It's probably for the best." She glanced down the opposite way toward the spiral center stairwell and wondered where the heck was the rush of hundreds of couples? Probably stealing kisses in some dark private corner. "Blast."

"Excuse me?"

"Sorry." She shook her head. "I was hoping to catch my... friend sooner than later, but with all these starry-eyed couples, strolling in on my own I'd stick out like a black sheep in a flock of white wooly relatives."

He chuckled then surveying the doors, and muttered, "Unless." He held up a finger and scanned the line of attendees and the people in charge of keeping others out. None looking nearly as careful about gate-keeping as they'd appeared to be a few minutes before. "I should introduce myself. I'm Devon. My friends call me Dev."

"My friends call me Angie." The dark gray eyes that had seemed filled with his own turmoil now danced with delight. She liked the change. It made her want to smile for the first time since her conversations with her mother had started two days ago. "Nice to meet you."

"Nice to meet *you*. Since you want in there, and I want in there, and we're both traveling alone..." he waited a beat for her to confirm. "And I'm guessing they've stopped actually looking for names on any list to keep the line moving," he extended his elbow, "what do you say we stroll in together looking like we own the place?"

She barked out a short laugh for the first time in days and curled her fingers around his proffered arm. Maybe this was a sign. "My mother always used to say, if you walk in like you own the place, no one will dare ask if you really do."

Smiling like the engaged couple they weren't, they strolled right past the greeters at the door, into the large room, and still holding onto his arm, she wondered how much of what she was up to was she going to have to explain to this friendly stranger.

First obstacle overcome. And if he did say so himself, not a bad ally. A waiter with a tray of champagne filled glasses paused at his side. "Would you care for some champagne?"

Dev shook his head, then as almost an afterthought turned to his new and unknowing comrade in arms.

She, too, shook her head.

"We also have chardonnay, cabernet, and Bahama Mamas," the man added.

The woman at Dev's side snapped her head back around from where she'd been carefully scanning the crowd. "I'm sorry, what?"

"Bahama Mama. It's the blue drink some waiters are carrying."

"Oh." She bobbed her chin and smiled brightly. "No, thank you."

With the slightest hint of a nod, the waiter moved on to the next couple.

"Do you see who you're looking for?" Dev asked.

Her attention once again surveying the attendees, she shook her head. "They might not be here yet."

"They?"

"Well. It's really him I want to see." Her gaze remained fixed on the strangers around them.

"I see." Even though he hadn't the slightest clue what her story was, he was sure of one thing, the guy that had let her get away was an idiot. Although, she could be an absolute shrew, or a flake, or a general pain in the rear, but her big blue eyes seemed too sharp to be a dunce, and her smile didn't fit the attitude of a shrew. His money was staying on the guy was an idiot.

Still debating with himself over the pros and cons of first impressions, the attractive brunette in question spun around and nearly collided with his chest for the second time in a very short while. "Are we going to make this a habit?"

Shaking her head, she took a short step in retreat. Then she stretched her arm out and grabbed one of those blue drinks from a passing waiter, took a too long sip, and muttered, "No."

Shame, too. He was starting to like the feel of her up against him. "I gather you found him?"

This time her head bobbed up and down. And she took another sip. "This is crazy."

He wasn't too sure which part of the last few minutes was the crazy part, but looking over her shoulder, he found himself wondering which *him* was her *him*, and then he wondered if her crazy was as bad as his crazy. Leaving his work behind on a moment's notice and boarding a cruise ship to chase down a full-grown man in order to convince him not to marry a near stranger certainly held its own goodly amount of crazy. A waiter with a tray of red wine crossed in front of him and he followed Angie's lead. Stretching his arm out, he snatched a glass from the tray without anyone missing a step. Downing a long, slow sip, he glanced over the rim of his glass and decided his story was crazy enough for both of them. After all, what other sane adult would chase down their parent this way?

CHAPTER FOUR

Oh, Lord, now what? Angie kept her gaze on her new… *friend's* collar bone. Though she wasn't terribly sure *friend* was quite the right word for a stranger who she'd sucked into helping her with her subterfuge and now was dangerously close to burying her face in his shoulder. This was a bad idea.

"Want to tell me why?"

"Huh?" Had he said something else she didn't hear? "I'm sorry, what?"

"Do you want to tell me why this is a bad idea?"

She knew if her eyes opened any wider they'd fall out of the sockets. "Did I say that out loud?"

An amused twinkle shone in his eyes. "You did."

Closing her eyes, she blew out a heavy sigh and then leveled her gaze with his. "I'm not the sort of person who doesn't look before I leap. If there's a plan to be made, I make it well in advance, and have a back plan, or two, in place. There's usually a timeline involved, and most likely a spreadsheet or two."

"Sounds familiar." That amused grin was back.

"Coming on this cruise was a bit… impulsive."

"Man, do I understand that. Even though many would argue that a full twenty-four hours to organize was not impulse, for me, it was ridiculously spur of the moment."

"Really?" He looked so sincere, and yet, she wondered if he was just trying to make her feel better.

He nodded. "Really. Why don't you tell me what you're up against?"

"Only if you promise not to laugh."

His forefinger extended, he drew an x across his heart

and then raised his arm to his side holding up two fingers. "Scouts honor."

"Were you ever a boy scout?"

"Card carrying." He had a really nice smile.

"My mother met some lothario." Angie didn't want to consider what could happen with the other television worthy possibilities. "She hasn't even introduced me to him. But here they are, running off to live happily ever after."

He muttered something that sounded an awful lot like, "Seems to be a run on that this week."

No clue what the man actually said, but no matter, she needed to focus on the task at hand. She still couldn't believe there were over three hundred couples on this ship waiting to get married. Shaking her head, she dared to look out to the crowd. "To make the situation even worse, from the little she would tell me, I found out that she's been buying him little... *trinkets* and she won't even consider a pre-nup. If the guy thinks she's loaded, oh boy, is he going to be in for a surprise."

"I know what you mean. My father is in the same situation and doesn't know it."

"You did say that, didn't you?" Her gaze drifted back toward him.

He nodded at her. "The gold-digger has already gotten him to give her a rock for her finger the size of Gibraltar, and when they get back home he'll be buying her a house in an extremely high rent district. I think it's a scam from A to Z, but without having met her, I can't do much to check her out."

"Oh, I am sorry. At least I'm only guessing this guy is after mom's money. I don't have any real evidence like you do. For all I know he could have a hundred other reasons that are even more frightening, but what I do know is it's really scary how easily my mother who has always been reasonable and sensible and my sounding board of good advice, can be taken in by one good con artist."

"I can't fathom how much more worried I'd be if it were my mom and not my dad in this mess."

"Oh, there she is." Angie turned, showing her back to her mother who now stood no more than twenty feet away. "I don't want her to see me yet. I'm not ready."

"I know how you feel." Dev took her elbow and ushered her across the large room to a quiet nook.

Backs to the wall and fruity drink glass in front of her face, as much for camouflage as courage, she was prepared to settle in and watch the lothario all night, or week. What she needed was his name and a better plan, or any plan at all. This flying by the seat of her pants wouldn't have gone so well if Dev hadn't been in the same boat. Figuratively speaking, that is. Although, maybe he could give her some good ideas on how to proceed with this crazy plan that wasn't fully a plan. "I'm curious. What's your plan?"

"Don't have one. I'm in the same situation as you. Just getting eyeballs on my father's intended for the first time, and hoping I'll be able to size the gold-digger up faster and much better than my dad did. Of course, I should probably start with her name."

"Yes, that's what I need." She set her drink on a nearby empty table and scanned the room for her mom in the distance, only to be surprised as all get out to see the two strolling once again in her direction. Had her mom spotted her only daughter? No, she couldn't have. Could she?

"You're looking a little green around the gills."

"I'm feeling a little green. Mom is coming this way with the lothario."

Dev stiffened. "How far away are they?"

"About thirty feet and closing the gap. I don't think they're going to stop anywhere along the way either. She seems to be looking for something. I can't get a good look at him in this light."

"How close now?"

"Twenty feet. Oh. They're chatting up another couple!" She inched a fraction to the right in an effort to let his tall frame shield her from her mother's line of sight. Now she could almost get a better glimpse of the man. If her mom would just turn a smidge, she'd stop blocking the happy couple from a clear picture of the... oh crud. Her mother shifted totally around and any second now would be staring straight at Angie. Her back to the wall, there was nowhere to go. She didn't have a choice. The oldest trick in the book always worked in the movies. It should work now too. Shouldn't it?

Panic as clear as the glimmering swimming pools on deck flashed in her eyes a moment prior to feeling the tug. Her fingers curled around his collar edge and before his mind could even begin to process what she was thinking, warm pliable lips pressed firmly against his.

The brief surprise shifted to shock and then the reality of the moment set in. It was quite nice. More than nice. She fit so perfectly against him that he forgot about his father, forgot about the gold-digger, and forgot about the panicked look she'd flashed him seconds before pressing against him. It felt like the most natural thing in the world to wrap his arms around her and pull her fully against him. So natural that he shifted his stance so she'd fit even more closely and completely forgot about the public around them. Until a rough and very loud voice echoed *Welcome to your Destiny*.

Angie stiffened in his arms and he knew she'd been reminded of the same thing he had. They weren't alone. Not only weren't they alone, they barely knew each other. Hell, he didn't even know her last name. He had no business kissing her like she'd really been his.

"Can you see them?" he muttered softly against her forehead. "Or are they still watching us?"

"Um." Her fingers released their hold on his shirt. "I…"

"That's why you kissed me. So your mother wouldn't recognize you?"

Her shoulders relaxed and she nodded. "They were coming toward us. I didn't know what to do. It always works in the movies."

"I can see why." He felt an odd urge to laugh. As if the joke was on him. "Can you see where she went?"

She paused a long moment before shaking her head. "I don't see her—them—anymore."

Inhaling a deep breath, he took a long step back and wished someone would pass by with a tray full of tall glasses of ice water. He could use one—or four. "I should probably look for my dad too."

Angie nodded. "What does he look like?"

Doing a quick survey of the couples surrounding them, Dev was a little surprised to see just how many people his father's age were planning a runaway wedding. "Destiny must specialize in seniors. Pop's a couple of inches shorter than me and has a full head of salt and pepper hair."

This time Angie's gaze scanned the crowd and frowned. "Oh my, I can see what you mean. There are quite a few people who fit your dad's description, and that doesn't include the people on the other side of the room."

Dev nodded. She was absolutely right.

"Please enjoy the drinks and the music..." The shift from music to words caught Dev's attention. Neither one of them had been listening to a single word the captain had said.

Just in case the man shared anything helpful, Dev and Angie remained still, quietly listening.

"And if we don't see you this evening at karaoke, we shall see you in the morning for game time." A band he had not noticed earlier began playing a peppy tune. Most of the invited guests remained for the free drinks and dancing, but grabbing hold of her hand, Dev moved to a spot where they could better see the lounge room doors and the few people leaving.

"May I interest you in another drink?" A waiter paused at their side.

Dev reached around to retrieve a glass of wine when his gaze fell on a familiar face. "Thank you," he told the waiter, and watched his father laughing at the edge of the dance floor. He waited for him to turn around so Dev could see the woman's face. "I found mine."

"Are they dancing?" Angie asked.

"I suppose you could call it dancing. They're barely

moving, and Pop is finding something terribly amusing."

"Which one are they?" Angie leaned into him, her gaze following the direction of his finger. "Oh. He's handsome."

Shifting to fully face her, Dev cleared his throat. "You sound surprised."

Angie turned, her hand on her chest, and her eyes wide. "Not surprised that he's handsome. I just think I was looking for someone a little older, and stodgier. The sort who might be more likely to fall for the schemes of a gold-digger."

His gaze narrowed and he shook his head. "Do you want to explain that again?"

"Not really." She chuckled softly. "I just hadn't expected him to be good-looking enough to have his pick of any nice woman. I guess I just always assumed gold-diggers preyed on balding men with low self-esteem."

"Too bad, I can't see her. The guy who is balding and stodgy is completely blocking her from view." Sighing, he returned his attention to the dance floor. Only his father and the gold-digger were no longer in the same spot. Blast. "My mother has been gone a lot of years. Part of me would like to believe that this woman is someone really special to finally make Dad show some interest in enjoying life again, but this whole set up really smells like a rat."

Angie turned around to watch the dance floor as well. "I don't see them any more."

"Nope." He glanced across the dance floor and scanned the tables that surrounded the area. "What about your mom?"

"Nope. But Mom doesn't like to dance."

A short while later, the crowd had begun to thin, and neither Dev nor Angie had spotted their respective parents again.

"Looks like we have no choice but to accept that they snuck out without our noticing." Angie set down the diet cola she'd ordered.

"Agreed."

"Have you got a plan yet?"

Dev shook his head. "Not yet."

"I am beginning to think that spying on my mother isn't going to work. I'm wasting precious time to convince her she's making a mistake."

"I was thinking the same thing. I only found Pop once and then promptly lost sight of him."

"The question is, do I call her room and talk to her in private, or do I wait for karaoke later and hope she won't kill me in a lounge filled with witnesses."

Dev let out a full belly laugh. Every serious situation required a little levity, and she'd just provided it for him. "Thank you."

"For what?" Her brow crinkled with honest confusion.

"Making me laugh."

"Oh." She waved him off. "Anytime."

She seemed casual but Dev got the impression she was feeling anything but. "If I know my father at all, he's off finding food. Could I persuade you perhaps to join me in a bite to eat? We could firm up a plan B before we come face to face with our parents."

"That is probably the smartest thing I've heard all day." Her stomach rumbled in agreement.

Once again, he extended his elbow for her to reach onto, and together they deciphered where they were in relation to the dining rooms and quickly made their way across the ship and into the massive hall.

"Oh, this is lovely." Still smiling, she looked around at all the people.

"Table for two or do you mind sitting with other guests?" the maitre d asked.

"Others is fine," Dev answered for both of them before looking to her for her input.

She nodded. "Fine with me."

"Very well. Follow me."

Single file, they followed behind the waiter and when he came to a stop at a larger table, one of the upright menus slid down exposing a silver haired man around his father's height and general features. For a fraction of a moment, Dev thought he'd stumbled onto his father and the gold-digger. Judging by the age of the bleached blonde at the older man's side, Dev may not have found his father, but he'd wager big bucks that the blonde saw plenty in the man's wallet. "On second thought," Dev turned to the waiter, "table for two, please."

CHAPTER FIVE

"I'll bite." Angie followed the maître d' back to the podium to assign a new seat. "What happened?"

"Nothing really. For a split second I thought that man at the table was going to be my father. It hit me that I really do need a plan before I run into him, and I'm not going to form one making polite conversation with two strangers at my side."

If he thought about it, three including her. "Why don't we skip this formal scene?" she suggested. "There's a great little pizza place upstairs and a handful of tables just outside on deck. It takes people a couple of days to scope out the pizza joint, so it probably won't be busy."

One eyebrow rose high seconds before the second one did the same. "You cruise a lot, do you?"

She laughed. "Hardly. But I was on this line's sister ship a couple of years ago for a friend's wedding. The pizza place was great for getting away from the crowds. And if there's one thing a cruise ship is always, it's crowded."

"Then pizza it is." Dev made their excuses to the dining supervisor and gestured for Angie to lead the way. "After you."

Across the promenade and up the elevator, neither said a word, but both had surveyed every inch of the massive ship. It wasn't the shooting fountains, zealous sales people hawking the goods inside their little shops, or pubs and snack spots in their paths that held their interest. What each of them studied carefully were the people. Scanning all the faces, looking for the two couples that had been their entire reason for coming aboard in the first place.

At the small pizza joint, seated at one of the few café

tables, Dev lifted his slice of pepperoni pizza. "If you'd chosen the one with pineapple I would have had to work this out on my own." Smiling, he took a bite.

"I can handle meats and veggies but plain cheese or pepperoni are my go to. Otherwise it stops being pizza."

Between bites, they discovered both lived in neighboring counties in a middle of nowhere state, both had grown up in small towns, both worked longer hours than they cared to admit, neither had taken a vacation in too long to count, both had benefited from happily married role models, and both had been blindsided by their parents' announcement they were running away to get married, probably to people intending to scam them out of their money.

"The grown up in me wants Mom to find someone. Understands that she's too young to spend the rest of her life alone."

Dev nodded.

"And I really do understand, and don't mind. At least, I don't think I do." Angie reached for her drink and took a sip.

"It's hard," Dev agreed. "Some days I still expect to find Mom in the kitchen and it's been forever since we lost her."

"There are a lot of things I could maybe overlook, but what bothers me is why marry so fast? Why no time to let me meet him?"

Swallowing his last bite, Dev nodded. "Exactly. Why not give me time to get to know the bride-to-be? What's there to hide?"

She leaned in and lowered her voice. "I wonder if any more of the weddings planned for this week are suspicious?"

"I honestly hadn't considered that. I just assumed my father was an isolated incident. Now hearing your story and seeing so many more couples, I wonder."

"Do you think this organized wedding company has something to do with both our parents rushing to marry someone they haven't known very long?"

"I honestly don't know. Everyone in the group we saw seemed perfectly normal. And even in love. I didn't notice anything odd. It doesn't fit with a whirlwind, let's hurry up and marry relationship. Though I have to admit, the little glimpse I caught of Dad, he did look awfully happy. Really seemed to be enjoying himself."

Now Angie felt guilty. Her mom had been smiling too. Not just a polite smile but the kind that reached all the way to her eyes. Even in the dimly lit and crowded room, Angie could tell her mother was having a good time. "So are we making too much of this?"

Dev shook his head. "Don't get me wrong. I want my dad to be happy and I don't want him to live the rest of his life alone, but this is just too fast. It doesn't feel right."

Good. Not being the only one to think that way made her feel a little better. A little less stupid for jumping on the first flight to Florida and splurging on a cruise cabin all to herself. "So if I know you and I are both right about this situation and our respective parents, why am I still afraid I'm going to be the one who comes up looking like a lunatic when I try one more time to tell my mother she's behaving like an adolescent?"

A grin spread across his face. "Safety in numbers."

"What?"

Elbows on the table, weaving his fingers together in front of him, he steepled two fingers. "We helped each other sneak into the welcome affair tonight. Why not stick together when we find our parent and then I can back you up and you can back me up."

"Sort of like moral support and a character witness all rolled into one?"

"Exactly." He nodded his head sharply.

She reached for her cola and felt her cheeks tug at the edge of her lips. "I like it. Safety in numbers. That's a plan I can get on board with. So we find our parent and then we'll help each other convince them that they've lost their minds."

"You may not want to phrase it that way when you talk to your mother."

"Right. If Mom's behaving like a teenager, she'll probably just dig her heels in even more just to be contrary." Tossing her napkin onto the paper plate, Angie leaned back in her seat. "If we run into them at tonight's karaoke, we'll have the element of surprise on our side. Otherwise, we could wait till morning and call. The desk won't give me my mother's room number but they will connect a phone call. Except, if I do that Mom will have time to shore up her excuses."

"I think the element of surprise is a good tactic. It's what got each of us this far. Now we have a more solid plan. The element of surprise and safety in numbers. It's a big ship, but if we can follow Destiny's itinerary, we should be able to find them."

"And no time like the present to continue the hunt." She pushed to her feet, taking her trash with her and dropping it into a nearby receptacle. She could do this. She had to find a way to convince her mother that this rushed marriage was a childish mistake. Maybe Dev was just the leverage she needed, or maybe it would just plain be more fun with a man who could make her forget her own name when he kissed her.

The small upper deck club had wonderful sea views even in the pitch of night. Dev made a path through the scattered tables and chairs until he and Angie could see the red corded area. Once again, the freestanding sign reminded guests that this was a private event reserved for Destiny's Destination Weddings. On the other side of the velvet rope representatives from the cruise line and the Destiny operation sat behind a table on either side of the entry way. The difference between this activity and the welcome party was that the staff appeared to be paying attention to who crossed into the area.

"Oh, dear." Angie's steps slowed. "Looks like we might need more than a little togetherness."

"Would you rather sit out here by the elevators? If they go in, we'll be able to see them."

"Unless they're already inside." Angie spun about and snapped her fingers. "Wait a minute. If they are checking off names from the Destiny group, Mom and I have the same last name. Maybe that's all we need to sneak in?"

"Same goes for me too." He stretched out his arm and wiggled his fingers at her. "Only one way to find out."

"Here goes nothing." Her hand slipped into his.

He could almost hear them holding their breath as they approached the roped off area.

Inside the velvet cords, a smiling brunette with plenty of bubble in her personality waved a pencil at a large book to her side. "These are all the songs we have available. Sign your name and your fiancées name on the line here, let us know what song you want to sing, and we'll notify you when it's your turn." Her hand swung back to point to a line on the binder in front of her with her pen.

"We're not singing," he said without consulting Angie.

"I'm sorry," the woman at the table looked perplexed, "didn't you get the activity description?"

Shaking his head was easy. Didn't matter that he wasn't *supposed* to get the instructions.

The brunette reached into a bag at her side and pulled out a double-sided page. "Glad I brought extra. For this couple's event, everyone who joins us needs to pick and sing one song. Part of building togetherness."

From where he stood, he could hear one of the cruise company staff mutter to another staffer beside him, "Or the last straw." Dev was inclined to agree. The way Angie's eyes popped, she clearly didn't want to do this anymore than he did.

The brunette nudged the song book in his direction. "You can take the binder with you and look it over, but don't take too long, we only have a few and are expecting a nice crowd."

In a single move, without letting go of her hand, he scooped the book up and steered them toward the back corner and up the steps to a small table with a view of the entire place.

"What are the chances they'll forget all about us?" Angie let go of his hand and slid into the half moon booth.

Slipping in beside her from the other side, his gaze lifted to the front table and the line of couples growing. "Slim comes to mind."

"This is ridiculous. Who ever decided that singing together—in public—brings couples closer?"

"I gather you can't carry a tune." He bit back a smile. "I wouldn't let that bother you. I don't think actually being able to sing is a requirement for karaoke."

She shook her head. "I sing just fine."

Something about the nonchalant response and the way her gaze danced about the room made him think maybe that wasn't the problem.

"I'm here to talk some sense into my mother, not entertain the masses."

A waiter came by and set a napkin in front of each of them. "What can I get you?"

"Diet cola please," Angie ordered, then returned her gaze toward the front door.

"Just ice water please." So far Dev hadn't seen any sign of his dad and he wondered if either of their parents would show up before they got roped into singing. "We probably should at least pretend to be looking for a song."

Her fingers already on the cover, she nodded. Great minds think alike. *Stall as long as we can* went through my mind too.

The brunette at the entry table stood, and pivoting in a near perfect semi circle, slowly surveyed the surrounding crowd.

Fingers tapping at the tabletop, Angie shook her head. "Wanna bet she's searching for the songbooks?"

"Never take a sucker's bet." Just for effect, in case anyone really was keeping tabs on them, he flipped a page back then forward again.

The waiter reappeared with their drinks and even though Dev didn't have a clue what was on it, continued flipping through the song lyrics pages.

Her gaze not moving from the lounge's entrance doors,

Angie took a long swallow of the drink and set the tall glass back down. "If she's not here, where could she be?"

It was all Dev could do not to spit out the first thing that came to mind. Somehow, Angie didn't seem the type to appreciate any suggestion of her mother and company letting nature take its course. "Maybe she's enjoying a late, uh, dinner."

"I suppose." Her gaze drifted around the room and back. "Any sign of your father?"

Dev shook his head. Even with his attention divided between the songbook, the cute way Angie nibbled on the edge of her lower lip while staring at the front door, and the growing crowd of soon-to-be-newlyweds mulling about, there was no sign of his father and the gold-digger. "Something tells me this may be a long night."

One of the uniformed crew trotted onto the small stage. "Welcome, Destiny couples. We're so glad to have you share your wedding adventure with us."

"Adventure?" Angie mumbled out of one side of her mouth. The same side she'd been nibbling on moments ago. "I didn't realize karaoke constituted adventure."

The man on stage continued, "What better way to build on the foundation of a lifetime than to make music in front of your fellow lovebirds."

"Oh, talk about a sugar overload," Dev muttered. Never mind a long night. If he couldn't convince his father, and quickly, that this whole spur of the moment wedding thing was a really bad idea, all this saccharin-induced couple bonding would make for a very long cruise.

"If you haven't told our team which song you want to perform, please take a minute and get on the list. I'm sure you've noticed tonight's choices are all about love. For our first performance tonight, we have Alice and Jeremy performing 'Don't Go Breaking My Heart'."

Fortunately, Alice and Jeremy both carried a decent tune. Still, there was no risk they'd be topping the charts anytime soon, but at least they weren't painful to anyone's ears. They weren't so lucky with the second tune. Dev vaguely remembered hearing the song in a movie when he was a kid, but the way the two singers cooed and batted their lashes and nuzzled cheek to cheek, he didn't doubt any minute they really would "Say Something Stupid Like I Love You."

Blowing out a heavy sigh, Angie kept shaking her head. "Mom is just going to have to wait till tomorrow. There's no way I'm getting up there and making a fool of myself batting cow-eyes at you." Her eyes suddenly widened and her head whipped around to face him. "Nothing personal or anything."

He almost burst out in a roar of laughter. For a second he'd thought she'd spotted her mother, then he realized she'd merely been concerned that she might have hurt his feelings. The idea of it was both uniquely entertaining and highly endearing.

Another set of couples came and went and Angie's gaze darted more desperately to the front door and back, followed by a vehement head shake.

The announcer returned on stage. "If you're having trouble picking a song, our team is quite good at this."

"Glad someone is," she muttered, once again looking to the door.

"So," the man continued, "when it's your turn, if you still haven't made up your mind, a song will be assigned to you. Makes for lots of fun and helps get us out of here before tonight's lounge act needs the floor back."

Most of the people in the room laughed with the man, but Angie's face went slightly ashen. "Assigned to us?" She mumbled so low he barely heard her.

"Are you okay?"

CHAPTER SIX

This was not what Angie had bargained for. She either needed to gct out of here and fast, or have something a lot stronger than a diet cola to drink. On the other hand, memories of four Heavenly Hazes and a very nasty headache the next morning was more than enough to convince her the only solution was to escape to her cabin and get a good night's sleep. The wedding was almost a week away. She could find her mother tomorrow.

"Are you feeling okay?" he repeated slowly.

Her fingers gripped the edge of the table. "I think I'm going to be sick."

"Sick bay disperses meds for motion sickness. Or patches, if you prefer."

"Not that kind of sick."

Dev studied her a little longer and a little harder than she was comfortable with. Truth was, it didn't take much to make her uncomfortable. Not that she was painfully shy or anything; after all, she was sitting at the table with an almost perfect stranger. One who she was going to barf all over his shoes if she didn't get her nerves under control. She'd simply grown accustomed, maybe too accustomed, to the solitude of working from home.

"Is it the singing?" he asked, surprise in his tone.

She nodded. Even though the audience was more accurate an explanation for the bees buzzing around in her stomach.

"After listening to that extremely sour rendition of 'Ain't No Mountain High Enough', and hearing the enthusiastic applause, I think it's safe to say this is not a very discerning audience."

"That doesn't help." This time she shook her head vehemently from side to side. Sometimes logic was totally irrelevant. "I can't do this."

"Okay."

Just *okay*. That was all he had to say? No convincing counter argument? No understated reprimand for unwarranted nerves? No instant analysis on the run? She took in his face. It was a nice face. She would have had to have been blind not to have noticed that before, but now that she was truly looking at him, it was definitely a nice face. And if she let herself relax and think about it, a kind face too. A face that didn't seem to mind the idea of singing in front of a decent sized audience. On key or off.

She sucked in a deep breath, blew it out slowly, and willed her nerves to get a grip. "I was a freshman in high school."

Casually leaning forward, Dev nodded, but didn't say a word.

"Just like all the other kids in my grade, anyone who tried out for the school play wound up in the chorus. Actually being able to sing was merely an added perk."

Her gaze remained on her fingers twirling the straw in her drink so he didn't bother reacting.

"That first year we did *Anything Goes*. I actually had to learn to tap dance." She smiled. "Was pretty good at it too."

"I bet."

Her gaze lifted to meet his. For a split second, she'd almost forgotten who she was telling this story to. She didn't bother to ask herself why, she just kept talking. "We had a lot of fun, so the following year I tried out again. I loved everything about the production and I even got to say a few lines. By my junior year I was an old hat at it. Had a slightly bigger role in *Grease*. No solos or anything, but I'd grown to feel right at home on stage. By now pretty much everyone knew I could carry a tune, and lots of people had told me that I would have made a better Sandy than Mary Ellen Zondervan. Honestly, deep down I agreed with them. So much so that when the school announced they would be doing *Beauty and the Beast* our senior year, I tried out for Belle."

She dared look up to see his nod of approval.

"It was actually amusing. One of the teachers who usually listened to each kid sing from his seat in front, walked around to stand at my side as if he thought I might have had a pocket recorder or something doing the singing."

"So you really can sing." It wasn't a question.

"Better than anyone realized. I got the part." She could tell by the quizzical look that took over his face, he had no idea where this story was going. She only wished she didn't know either. "I loved the costumes. Some of the quick changes were fast and tricky, but all the test runs went great."

"So far, so good."

"Yeah. Everything was perfect. Right up to the moment I found myself alone on the stage, the spotlight on me, I opened my mouth, and," she breathed deeply, "nothing came out."

"Nothing?"

"Not a sound. Not a squeak, not a whimper, not a note. Nothing. When the rest of the cast realized something was wrong, the kid playing Gaston came out onto the stage and ad-libbed something to get close enough to me. He asked what was wrong and my mouth moved but nothing came out. I simply couldn't talk. He signaled to lower the curtain and when our math teacher, pseudo director came running over, I couldn't talk to him either. It was Gaston who told our director that I'd lost my voice. One of the other kids filled in for me and I went home and stayed home for over a week."

"You didn't try to do the performance the next night?"

A fair question. She shook her head. "There was no point. My voice conveniently remained AWOL until the morning after the last performance."

"I'm sorry."

"Not as much as I was. I let everyone down."

"The other girl didn't do a good job?"

Angie shrugged. "Well enough, but it wasn't fair to her or anyone else. I let everyone down."

"You said that already. And for the record, I don't agree."

"I don't believe in false modesty, nor do I believe in masking failure. I blew it. I am very clearly terrified of singing in front of a crowd. And this," she waved her arm widely, "definitely constitutes a crowd."

"Probably fewer than your high school auditorium." His voice held a bit of uncertainty. He was taking a wild guess and knew it.

"I wouldn't bank on that." She slurped the last sip in her cola.

"This singing thing is stupid. You shouldn't have to do it."

Another waiter passed by with a tray of mixed drinks and she had the ridiculous thought to ask if they had any Chianti.

Dev eyed another approaching waiter. "Would you like one? I believe the waiter said this one is called Bailey's Banana Colada. A little drink could help take the edge off the prospect of singing, and help you get a good night's sleep. Well rested, you can focus on approaching your mother tomorrow."

Her mind said no, her head turned slowly from side to side, but when her mouth opened, the words *I suppose one BBC won't hurt* came tumbling out. The next thing she knew, she'd sipped down half of the tasty concoction, except her nerves continued as frazzled as a cat in a room of rockers, and she still hadn't spotted her mother coming through the doors. A young couple belted out another screechingly loud chorus-ending *ah-ha*, more off key than the one before, and the audience responded with thunderous hoots and cheers. Either Dev was absolutely right and the audience wasn't very discerning, or the almost empty BBC was actually relaxing her perspective. She was almost tempted to order another when common sense shook its head at her. One wouldn't hurt anyone, and maybe neither would two, but she wasn't about to test that theory. Not again.

One of the uniformed staff approached the table and reached for the book. "Have you picked your song yet?"

Angie shook her head with the fervor of a happy dog

wagging his tail, but just like that night years ago on stage, no words came out.

"I'm afraid we haven't." Dev nudged the book to the man.

"No problem." The guy tucked it under his arm, and swiped at his tablet. "What are your names?"

If she wasn't sure it would only succeed in drawing more attention to them, Angie would have slid off the seat and under the table. Was the guy asking about the singing, or checking if they were really part of this group?

"Miller." Dev slid his hand from the table onto the Angie's hand and squeezed. "But my fiancée isn't wanting –"

The guy cut him off, scanning the list from the sign-in table. "Here you are. We can pick a song for you. Happens all the time. And good thing too. You're up next."

Before Dev could utter another word about Angie not wanting to sing, the guy scurried off with the book, waving it up at his colleagues as though it were the Stanley Cup. This time Angie considered sliding under the table for real. She did not want to do this.

If there was such a thing as a color more pale than white, Angie was it. He'd never seen the color literally drain from a person's face before. "I'm sure once I walk over and explain that we're leaving early, all will be fine." Big blue eyes stared blankly at him and he wondered if maybe she was about to pass out. "Angie?"

She blinked. "I'm being an idiot, aren't I?"

That wasn't the response he'd expected. "I wouldn't—"

"No. You're too nice to say that. High school was a crazy long time ago, and I should be able to stand up there and sing a few notes in front of a few people."

He didn't want to contradict her at a time like this, but he was pretty sure the crowd gathered tonight wouldn't be considered "a few people" by anyone.

"I should do this." It was debatable whether she was talking herself into it, or trying to convince him.

Either way, he wasn't sure this was a very good idea. "We can't be the first couple who backed out of singing."

"I'm sure we're not. But I'm also pretty sure we're the only people who have ever sneaked in to one of these events, two including earlier tonight, in order to find their crazy parents and possibly expose the group for scammers taking advantage of lonely old people."

When she put it that way, maybe drawing attention to themselves wasn't in their best interest. Then again, having her freeze up on stage—or worse, pass out—wasn't exactly inconspicuous behavior. "I don't know."

She grabbed hold of his hand again and squeezed. "Let's do this."

Oh, this woman was full of surprises. Or crazy. The last *ah-ha* carried across the lounge, both sour *and* off key. So much so that Dolly and Kenny would have cringed. The announcer trotted onto the stage playing jump rope with the microphone's cord. Maybe if they were really lucky the guy would trip and create enough commotion to kill the time left till they were done for the night, except Dev's chances of winning the lottery were probably higher.

Hands still entwined, her grip almost tight enough to cut off circulation, they eased their way out of the booth as their names reverberated around the room. The same people who had cheered excitedly for every couple so far regardless of skill, applauded loudly for them too.

If Angie walked onto the small stage any more slowly, she'd be walking backwards. Ducking his head so his mouth was within inches of her ear, he whispered, "Are you sure?"

Except for squeezing her eyes tightly shut, she didn't say a word. This was not going to be pretty.

The screen switched on, the music started, and the crowd recognized the tune a few seconds before he did. Someone whistled loudly, another hooted, and the energy in the room climbed. There probably wasn't a generation of music lovers who didn't know that tune. At least the first lines were his. Maybe that would put her at ease. He squeezed her hand again and she didn't move. *Or not.*

Too late to back out now. The first words flashed on the screen and when the notes lined up, he leaned into the mic and started. "I've got chills…" He felt Angie inch forward and hoped it was a good sign. By the time he sang "electrifying" he realized Angie was staring blankly at the crowd and once again he leaned into her side and softly whispered, "Close your eyes."

Instantly her eyelids slammed shut. He squeezed her hand again and without looking at the screen, she barely squeaked out, "You better shape up." Not really singing, barely talking. Though it didn't seem to matter, the crowd was on the edge of their seats and by the chorus it sounded like the entire place had chimed in with them. He supposed the ones practically dancing in their seats had probably been transported back to their own high school days when the film had first released.

The shift in beats signaled the end of the chorus, and to his surprise he felt Angie's hand slip out of his. Mentally he braced himself to either sing falsetto as she ran off the stage, or put rusty CPR skills from his lifeguard days to use. Instead, still facing him instead of the audience, eyes still closed, feet glued to the stage, she curled her finger at him, and not till she'd reached the word *affection* did he realize she was no longer whispering, but actually singing. Not over the top loud, but at least the crowd could hear her. And they were loving their walk down memory lane. That or the fact that he and Angie were probably the first couple to actually sing on key.

He'd sung his next line a little stronger than he had before and was rewarded when her eyes popped open and taking a half step away from him, she tipped one shoulder at him and belted out the next bantering line. He had no idea where the stage frightened woman he'd shared a drink with had gone, but this gal was killing it. Apparently all those folks back in her high school were right—she made a great Sandy.

When the last *oo hoo hoo* was sung, the audience was

on their feet, applauding and hooting and hollering, and once again holding hands, he and Angie took a bow. To his surprise, she was grinning widely and her cheeks were flushed in a good way, not like someone about to keel over.

"You were great," he told her over the still cheering crowd. "A few times I almost forgot to sing my part."

"Thank you. Frankly, I'm a little stunned."

He wasn't going to mention so was he. Sliding into the seat beside her, he reached for a glass of water and downed it in one very long gulp. "I suppose we got lucky they picked a song you didn't need to see the Teleprompter to know the lyrics."

Lips pressed tightly together, her head bobbed slowly as a hint of a smile widened into a full-blown grin. "I nailed it, didn't I?"

"Absolutely." He smiled back at her. "Better than nailed it."

Water glass in hand, she took a quick sip then raised it in a silent toast. "To Mary Ellen Zondervan. Eat your heart out."

"To Mary Ellen." He raised his glass alongside hers. This woman was definitely unpredictable. If he could straighten his father out quickly, and she could do the same with her mother, maybe this trip wouldn't be so bad after all.

CHAPTER SEVEN

Angie swallowed a long sip of water. "Wish Mom had been here to see me. She's never going to believe it."

"Yes, I will."

Good thing Angie hadn't taken another sip or she would have spit the water clear across the table. "Mom!"

Arms crossed, Julia Cannon tapped her foot dramatically. "And what may I ask are you doing here?"

Angie looked over her mother's shoulder. She seemed to be alone. Could Angie be so lucky that they'd already had a fight and come to their senses? "Where's what's his name?"

"Not that it's any of your business, but he's gone to hunt down something for my headache. I was on my way to my cabin to lay down when the singing drew me in." She flipped her hand, palm open at her daughter. "Your turn."

Oddly enough, even though Angie expected to have this conversation with her mother, having her mom standing in front of her very much the way she would have when Angie was ten years old and had just used her mother's good cloth scissors to cut construction paper, left Angie equally at a complete loss for any suitable explanation.

Her mom shook her head slightly and blew out a slow breath that said way more about what she thought of running into her daughter than any words could. "While you think of a good reason for not telling me you were coming on this cruise," her mom's expression softened and the edges of her mouth barely tipped upward in the slightest hint of a smile, "you were fantastic. Better than fantastic. You killed it!"

Angie considered herself to have a healthy amount of self-esteem. She was average on the pretty scale, had done well in school, made a nice living now, and was blessed with good friends, but none of that mattered when she was standing on a public stage under a spotlight in front of a room filled with strangers. Healthy seemed woefully insufficient. Especially when added to her one major performance debacle. Hearing the praise from her mom felt good. Really good. "You really think so? I didn't look ridiculous?"

The hint of a smile blossomed into a full-blown grin. The familiar glint of pride Angie had often seen in both her parents' eyes when she was growing up shone brightly. "Aw, baby, I really do."

"Told you so." Dev flashed a cheeky grin that made her actually giggle.

"Thank you both." She wasn't sure she'd have the nerve to try it again, but it felt good to have left that long ago failure truly behind her.

"So," her mom waved a hand at Dev, "are you going to at least tell me who this fellow is?"

"I'm sorry." Angie sat up straighter. "Mom, this is Dev." She gestured from one to the other. "Dev, this is my mother, Julia."

Her mom bobbed her chin. "Nice to meet you."

"Likewise."

"So," her mother pivoted, focusing a once again steely gaze on Angie. "What is this all about?"

Dev tipped his head and raised his brow in a silent gesture that clearly said, *the ball is in your court.*

"I'm here for you, Mother. Why don't you join us?"

Dev shifted, ready to stand. "I could—"

With a raised hand, Angie cut him off. "Please stay. I could use some rational perspective."

"Can't argue with that," her mother muttered, slipping into a chair beside her. "I'm afraid if you want to be my maid of honor, I doubt the organizers will agree. I already explained to you before that couples weren't even allowed to bring guests or their own witnesses. The group is simply too large. Perhaps we can find some nearby viewing spot you can at least watch from."

"I'm not here to stand up for you, Mom. Though normally, for the record, I would be honored. I'm here because you simply can't be serious about marrying a man you've only known for a few weeks."

"Haven't you ever heard of love at first sight?"

"Seriously, Mom."

"Oh, honey, I knew your father was the man for me the moment he tripped over my handbag and then proceeded to trip over his own words apologizing for something that had clearly been my fault. When you're all grown up, a person doesn't need much time to know what they do and don't want. At my age, I don't have time to waste."

"I wish you'd stop saying 'at my age' all the time. You are not that old."

"Wait till you get to be my… well, you know."

"Mother." Angie hadn't meant to whine, but frustration got the better of her and the whiney teen in her just slipped out. "We're not talking about a dinner date. This is marriage. Something that with the best of intentions and years of dating doesn't bode well for over 50% of the population. You haven't a chance in hell with only two weeks under your belt."

"I'm sorry to point this out." Her mom gently lowered her hand over Angie's. "But it's my chance to take. Not yours."

Thrusting back against her seat, Angie sighed and resisting the urge to pinch the bridge of her nose and stave off an oncoming headache of her own, she smiled at Dev. "Maybe if you explain to her why running off to marry a man you've only known for two weeks is beneath her, that she deserves better, she'll listen."

Dev cleared his throat and leaned forward. "I know that this is really none of my business."

"Agreed," her mother said politely. Stern, but polite.

"But I must admit, I see where your daughter is coming from. I know I don't have as much life experience as you, and that perhaps your instincts are better than mine, but that doesn't negate the odds."

"At least you agree I have good instincts."

He smiled but didn't stress he'd said perhaps. Angie was going to give him extra diplomacy points for that one. "Have you thought about other potential issues? How much do you know about this man's finances? Is he looking for a free ride? Does he have debts out the wazoo that he expects his new bride to pay? Does he have some hidden addiction: gambling, women," Dev raised a suggestive brow at her, "maybe even drugs? It's not uncommon to find adults addicted to prescription medications."

For a few seconds, the way her mother paused, considering his words, Angie wanted to slap him on the back and cheer. All good points. And all too real a potential for a miserable outcome.

"He knows I'm a woman of meager means. I have my savings, sufficient but not substantial, and so does he."

"Who paid for this trip?" he asked.

"We each paid our own way." Her mom's shoulders straightened and she pushed off the table to stand. "I appreciate your concern."

"I love you, Mom, but Dev is right. There are so many red flags we haven't even begun to discuss."

Her mom patted her daughter's hand again. "I know you love me and I appreciate that. But that headache is getting worse and I really would like to go lay down so I don't miss out on tomorrow's activities. If you'd like to join us for breakfast, without the lectures, we're having the buffet at 8am. I know you're worried, but it will all be fine. I promise."

"Mom."

"Really, dear." Her mother blew her a kiss, gave a weak wave to Dev, and strolled out of the lounge the same way she might have gone for an afternoon walk, not a care in the world.

The element of surprise had come into play, but not in her favor, and safety in numbers hadn't gone so well either. Which meant all Angie had to do was come up with a new and brilliant plan to make her mother see the light. If only she knew how.

"She sounds like my father." Dev watched Angie's mother walk away. Even tired, the woman still stood tall. There wasn't a lick of confusion or doubt in the steely gaze that had followed his every word. Something told him that she'd considered all of those possibilities herself, and probably a few more.

"How so?"

"Convinced life and love are going to have a fairy tale ending despite the odds." He'd thrown all those very same arguments at his father and the older man had been just as stubborn. A pang of regret at bursting his father's bubble pricked at him. This must be what parenting was like. Doing what's best for your kid in the long run, even if it was going to make them unhappy in the here and now. He should have thanked his mother more often.

"Two weeks just isn't long enough. My mom may have fallen for Dad on day one, but they dated a year before he proposed and it was another six months before the wedding."

If only his father would take a year to get to know the gold-digger and let the dust settle. Even dating Goldie for a few months would be enough time to at least prepare a pre-nup in case his dad didn't see the light before the wedding, but this way there simply was no time. He turned to his partner in crime. "So now what's your plan?"

"I'll start with breakfast. I need to meet this guy. Find out anything I can. And then, depending on what I discover, I'll come up with a better plan."

"Better?"

"Anything has to be better than the conversation we just had." She took the last sip of water and set the empty glass near the edge of the table for a passing waiter to refill, then turned to fully face Dev. "And you?"

"That brief conversation was a bit of an eye-opener. If my dad is going to be as tough to convince as your mother, I'm going to need some strong coffee before I come face to face with him and Goldie."

"Goldie?"

"The gold-digger."

"Of course." She bit back a smile.

"Assuming that, like your mother and her friend, my dad and Goldie are following the schedule closely, the first activity doesn't start until nine o'clock. That will give me enough time to get my caffeine infusion before I have to call Dad."

"I hadn't thought of that. Maybe I should hit up coffee before I meet with Mom."

"If you'd like reinforcements?" He let the words hang. So far today they had helped each other sneak into events they didn't belong at, hidden behind one delicious kiss, brought down the house—so to speak—and perhaps a few old ghosts, and joined forces in an effort to convert her mother. The only failure of the day being the latter, but tomorrow there would be no need to sneak, or hide, or collude. He was no longer needed. Shame, too. He hadn't enjoyed any of the few social outings in his recent past as much as he had those few minutes on stage with Angie.

"If you're volunteering to back me up again, I won't turn you down. Convincing Mom to listen to reason isn't going to be easy."

"Consider me volunteered. Shall we meet at the buffet at, say, seven-thirty?"

"Seven-thirty it is. And on that note." She pushed to her feet. "I having a feeling tomorrow is going to be a long day and I'm going to need plenty of sleep to make it through."

Dev stood beside her. "Yeah, it's been a long day for me too. A bit of shut eye sounds great." Too bad something deep in his gut told him sleep wasn't going to come easy tonight.

CHAPTER EIGHT

Ever since working from home, Angie rose every morning at six like clockwork. Didn't matter whether it was daylight savings time or not, if the sun was awake or not, she was up and ready to go. This morning the clock screamed seven and she sprang out from under the sheets like a cat with its tail on fire.

At exactly seven twenty-seven she stepped off the elevator onto the upper deck with the buffet restaurant to one side and all the pool activities to the other. She'd managed to shower, dress, do her hair, brave the crowds of hungry passengers trudging along, and arrive at her scheduled meeting place in almost half the time it would normally take her.

"Good morning." The sound of Dev's husky morning voice sent shivers up her arms.

"If you say so."

"Rough night?" He chuckled.

She shook her head and started for one set of double doors. "Overslept. Rushing is never a great way to start a day."

"No." He grabbed a tray from the start of the coffee aisle and scanned the massive room with floor to ceiling windows all around. "No wonder people gain weight on vacation."

Following his gaze, she had to agree. Already she spotted several stations that were too tempting to resist. "I think there's a spinach and mushroom omelet with my name on it."

"I'll get something easy and find us a table."

She nodded, grabbing a couple of warm cinnamon buns

on her way to the omelet station. At least she was mixing protein with her carbs. That had to count for something. "See you in a few." Once her tray was full, it didn't take long to spot Dev at the far end, backlit by the morning sun.

"Eating for four?" He glanced from the eggs and bacon and hash browns and cinnamon buns plated in one hand to the coffee mug in the other.

"Comedian." Placing her breakfast on the table, one dish a time, she set the tray aside. "Breakfast is the most important meal of the day."

"That's what they say." Judging by the small bowl of fruit and scrambled eggs in front of him, she could see why the guy looked so fit. Probably never had to think about carbs.

"Do you like Italian food?"

His gaze popped up at her, a quizzical dimple between his brows. "Yeah."

"What's your favorite?"

"Lasagna."

"Eat it a lot?"

He shrugged.

"It's not fair."

"Okay, I give. What are we talking about?"

"Metabolism. Why some people—like you—have one, and others—like me—not so much."

This time his gaze slowly drifted down to her sandaled feet and back up again. "At the risk of getting slapped, your *metabolism* looks just fine."

"I wasn't fishing for compliments."

"I know, but that doesn't change the facts." He set his fork down on his near empty plate. "What brought all this on?"

"Just debating when I can squeeze in a few extra workouts on this floating hotel. I'd like to fit in my clothes when I get home."

"Now I get it. I hit the gym an hour ago. It's the price anyone who loves lasagna pays."

She hadn't expected that.

"Devon?" A tall man with salt and pepper hair and a

coffee mug in his hand hovered beside them.

Seconds before he pushed to his feet, Dev sucked in a deep breath and plastered on a plastic smile. "Good Morning, Pop."

"What in heaven's name are you doing here?" Dev's father sputtered in that parental tone that carried Dev back to his days as a wayward teen.

"Angie and I were just having breakfast. Won't you join us?" Dev didn't dare look over his shoulder for Goldie. To deal with her too, he'd need a second cup.

"Yes. Please." She smiled.

"Angie, this is my father, Raymond."

"It's very nice to meet you." His dad smiled politely at her then turned back to his son. "I'm expecting someone soon, but until then—"

No sooner was the man settled in the seat beside Dev when Angie popped up from her chair. "I'm going to grab a quick glass of juice. Does anyone want something?"

He and his dad shook their heads.

"I won't be long."

The two sat in silence as Angie scurried past the crowds to the fresh juice station. Whether she was suddenly thirsty or simply wanting to give Dev a few minutes to lay the groundwork with his dad, he didn't know, but assuming the latter, he appreciated her thoughtfulness.

"I didn't realize there was someone special in your life. You should have told me." His father took a short sip from his mug.

"Special?" Dev blinked and followed his father's gaze to where Angie stood pouring a glass of juice and his only partly caffeinated brain kicked into gear. His father thought he'd brought Angie on the cruise. "Angie and I met on board."

The pleasant expression on his father's face fell. "Then, young man, what are you doing on my ship?"

"It's not exactly your ship. And I think you know darn well why I am here."

Glass in hand, Angie slid back into her seat. "A few more days of fresh squeezed juice, and I may never be able to buy concentrate again."

"My wife used to squeeze fresh orange juice for breakfast every Sunday."

The unexpected memory brought a smile to Dev's face. "She did spoil us."

"That she did." His father took another slow sip of the hot coffee and cradled the cup in both hands. "I know you are not happy with my plans, but I think it bears repeating, this does not change how I felt about your mother."

"Pop—"

"No." His father held his hand up. "In all the sky-is-falling scenarios you lambasted me with the other night, no matter how much I tried to assure you that I am not marrying a man in disguise, a green card seeking foreigner, or a gold-digging bimbo—"

"Really, Pop—"

"Let me finish. You need to accept that your father is not a doddering old fool, and is not being taken advantage of by some scheming female."

"Dad, I want you to find someone. Really I do. But not some internet scammer."

"This is not a scam. We're just going round in the same circles. If you came on board to convince me to change my mind, then you'd better plan on enjoying a well deserved vacation because otherwise you've wasted your money." His dad glanced at Angie and with a grin and a raised brow, tipped his head toward his son. "I think I'm going to take a walk around and see if I can find my Russian man pretending to be a woman."

"Ha, ha." Dev responding dryly. "Very funny."

His father chuckled and patted his shoulder. "I couldn't resist."

Once his dad was out of earshot, Angie leaned forward. "I didn't realize that your father and Goldie met on the internet."

"Sometimes I think that's the only way people meet nowadays anyhow, but yes."

Lips pressed tightly together, she shook her head. "The more I hear about our parents' situation the more I can't help but wonder if this organization isn't really a scam behind the whole thing. I mean, so many mature couples. Easier targets. Of course not all are being scammed, but I wonder just how many other couples here met on the internet and are marrying very quickly without really knowing who they're promising to love, honor, and obey."

"And finance." Dev sighed. "I suppose if we make nice and talk to some of the couples, we might be able to find more people being duped and show this is part of a bigger scheme, but we can't possibly talk to all the wedding couples. Besides, I keep circling around to the cruise line. I'm willing to believe this Destiny's Destination set up is nothing more than a scam, but I have a hard time believing a large cruise line wouldn't have vetted an organization like that touting their line."

She sat back in her seat. "I thought about that. There does seem to be a great deal of separation of Destiny and the ship. So, I'm not so sure the cruise line has all that much to do with it."

"But I'm still wondering about Destiny. There's a lot of money changing hands around here." Who knew that many people were meeting online and wanting a fast and small destination wedding?

"There you are." Angie's mom came up beside her daughter, and smiling, leaned over to kiss the top of her head. "Did you get a good night's sleep?"

"Like a rock. Almost couldn't get out of bed."

"Really? My early bird?" Her mother's smile took over her face and an almost mischievous twinkle appeared in her eyes. "You must have had *some* night.

"No." Angie shrugged. "I hit the sack right after you left."

Looking at Dev, her mother rolled her eyes and heaved a soft sigh. Dev, on the other hand, bit back a grin. Unlike Angie, he had not missed her mother's innuendo. Still, it was refreshing getting to know someone as straightforward and down to earth as Angie who looked at the world through innocent eyes.

"I should take a walk around to see if my fiancé is here yet."

The word had Angie cringing behind her mother's back.

"Oh. Look. Here he comes." Julia Cannon leaned back slightly near her daughter and mumbled just loud enough for him to hear, "Isn't he handsome?" Then she snapped around quickly. "Not that your father wasn't handsome. I'm just saying, how often does a woman get lucky in love twice in a lifetime?"

"Yes." Angie plastered on a plastic smile. "Twice."

Dev took a chance and reached across the table, folded her hand in his and squeezed, quickly letting go before her mother or anyone else noticed. He knew he'd made the right choice in offering his reassurance when the more sincere, though slightly disheartened smile beamed up at him.

"There you are," an all too familiar voice announced from just behind him.

Julia and her expected beau fell into a quick embrace and already holding hands, turned to face Dev and Angie.

"For heaven's sake, young lady. Close your mouth or you'll catch flies."

Angie's mouth snapped shut, but her gaze remained fixed on the man standing beside her mother.

"Didn't your mother teach you it's not polite to stare?" his father snapped at him.

Dev turned to Angie and only one thing popped into his mind. "I'll have to stop referring to her as Goldie."

CHAPTER NINE

"This is your Angela?" Raymond Miller looked from Angie to her mother.

Eyes wide with surprise, Julia nodded at her fiancé. "And this is your Devon?"

Angie had no idea why it had not occurred to her that the sudden engagements and impending weddings that she and Dev wanted to undo could be one and the same, but it hadn't. Out of the hundreds of couples on this ship with one united goal, the odds just hadn't been there. And her mother was many things to many people, but gold-digger was most definitely not one of them. "I think I need something stronger than orange juice."

Dev spoke to Angie, but kept a casual eye on her mother. "I was just thinking the same thing."

Suddenly, everything seemed even more complicated than before. Considering how worried Dev was about a gold-digger being after his father's money, odds were pretty good that the man her mother wanted to marry wasn't a swindler. Still, that barely gave Angie even a tiny bit of relief. She was still very much on edge. There was still the matter of the very brief and very limited personal interaction that had hardly been in existence long enough to call a friendship, never mind a relationship. The unbridled determination to not use a pre-nup. Even if Dev's father wasn't after her money, not that her mother had very much, without the pre-nup that her mother had made perfectly clear that she had no intention of signing, financial disaster was still a very real possibility when the inevitable demise of the marriage arrived and divorce papers were signed.

"I don't see why you two are mumbling." Ray shot a

pointed glare in his son's direction. "You can clearly see that she's not a Russian man, not a gold-digger, and not a con artist. What do you know," his tone fluctuated with the lilt of sarcasm, "the sky isn't falling."

"Raymond," her mom softly censured.

The older version of Dev softened his stance. "Sorry, dear."

Aw, hell. This was not what Angie wanted to see. She didn't want a sweet cute couple behaving with mutual respect. She wanted a clear-cut bad guy who she could easily expose and save her mother from a colossal mistake worthy of a hormone driven teen with the proverbial stars in her eyes.

Julia Cannon glanced at her watch. "Oh heavens. We've only got fifteen minutes to eat before we need to leave."

"We're in luck." His dad smiled. "There's enough choices here to have a hearty breakfast in ten."

Her mom giggled—yes, giggled—gently tapped Dev's dad on the arm, and happily followed him toward the food without so much as a be-right-back or don't-wait-on-us. This was feeling more and more difficult with every passing hour.

Dev kept his gaze on their parents chatting in the distance, laughing, leaning in for private exchanges, and piling food high on their plates. "They're definitely in that merry infatuation stage. The one that sucks people into doing stupid things."

"We clearly need to regroup."

"We?" A brow arched high on Dev's forehead.

"Yes. We. Unless you've changed your mind about Goldie?"

"That's not fair. You know I thought your mom was a nice lady last night. And so far she hasn't done anything to change my mind about that, so the name no longer fits. But that doesn't mean that I think she and my dad should be getting married."

"So, as I was saying, where does that leave us? Can I assume the fact that you thought a gold-digger was after your father's money means that he has the means to take care of himself and possibly a wife?"

Dev nodded.

"That's what I figured. So, there's no point in texting my neighbor Jo with your dad's name. She's not going to be able to find any dirt on him to convince Mom that her life would be at risk with him. Never mind prove he's after her money. So how the hell do I get her to slow down?"

"And that is the question of the day."

"Uh oh. Here they come. That was fast."

"He's a stickler for punctuality."

"So is Mom."

"A match made in heaven," Dev muttered softly.

"We'll have to pick this up later."

Dev nodded and her mother came to stop at Angie's side. His dad, only a few steps behind, took the empty seat beside Dev. Though the casual way they locked gazes between bites of bacon and eggs was teetering somewhere between totally adorable and unpleasantly nauseating.

Waving a fork in Dev's direction, his dad tore his gaze away from Julia. "We're heading up to the game room. A little casual play time."

Dev blinked hard. Angie had the feeling he was trying to avoid rolling his eyes.

"Yes," Julia beamed. "We're not sure if we're going to join the whist teams or the Scrabble players."

"Maybe someone will have a Trivial Pursuit game going." Ray smiled at her mom.

"Oh, that would be nice." Somehow her mother grew even happier.

This was almost more than Angie could take, but tagging along made the most sense to her. She caught a glimpse of Dev from the corner of her eye and decided on the spot. "I'm in."

Dev's head snapped around. Taking Angie in for all of ten seconds, he nodded. "I'm in too."

Another couple of minutes and the four of them had finished their hurried breakfast, stood and made their way to the elevators and the game room. Angie followed in step behind her mom. If she ever had kids of her own, she would promise each and everyone that she would never do anything as crazy and foolhardy as her mother. She was so never marrying a man she'd only known two weeks. Love at first sight. Hogwash.

So far the morning was whizzing by. They'd had one heck of an eye opening breakfast, and a surprisingly fun time playing poker. Especially for Angie whose memory for numbers had her winning more than her share of hands. Next on the schedule, the dance lesson. Anxious to get started, her mom and Raymond had moved on to the class while she and Dev finished their last hand of cards. From the size of the larger crowd, either the subject or the later time of day held more appeal. Spotting her mother took a few minutes. "Over there. By the bar."

"Don't you look like the cat who swallowed the canary," her mother teased and Angie felt the heat rush to her cheeks.

"Your daughter is an honest to goodness card shark."

"Really?" Dev's dad nodded at Angie.

"Oh, yes." Julia Cannon clapped her hands together. "When she was a little girl, she could remember what cards had been dealt, played, and predict what was most likely to be dealt next."

"Really?" This time Raymond Miller's eyes widened, his brows rose higher on his forehead and his voice went up a notch.

Dev shifted his attention to her. "Well, that would certainly explain a lot."

Angie hadn't thought about that ability for a long while. Her keen memory for what had been played and to retain numbers was probably the key reason why she and her grandmother had enjoyed watching the television version of the Concentration game, and why she'd gotten her degree in accounting. "It's more helpful with games like rummy or whist."

The background music shifted from easy listening to something with a bit more tempo at the same moment one of the crew tapped the microphone garnering the attendees' attention. "Find your partner as we'll be starting with the simple Texas Two Step."

The couples lined up, forming a circle within a circle.

"I want everyone to face starboard." When most of the people turned one way or the other but not all in the same direction, the crewmember tried again. "I have a better idea, everyone turn toward my left side."

More people turned, some facing his left, some not.

"That would be my other left." His joke fell flat as some turned to face the correct way, and others who already were, spun around in the wrong direction. As more crew members descended onto the large dance floor, the vision of white uniformed people spinning and turning grown adults to face the same direction gave new meaning to the old cliché herding cats.

A couple of dancers from the ship's nightly musical production stood in the center of the group demonstrating the simplicity of the traditional Texas dance. The idea would have been helpful if the two were on a platform, but at the same level as they were, blocked by forty or more couples, they could probably have skipped the effort.

Even without music, Angie could already tell with Dev as her partner, she was going to very much enjoy the next sixty minutes. Standing this close, flashes of last night's kiss replayed in her mind. She could almost feel her lips tingling still.

"A penny for your thoughts?" Dev asked softly.

"Not worth that much." Angie made her best effort at a casual shrug and hoped her cheeks didn't betray her for being caught daydreaming about her dance partner's kissing skills.

His brows drew together and he shook his head. "I don't believe that for a minute."

"And here we go." Saved by the crewmember waving his arm up in the air, and a decidedly country tune that began playing at the same time the staff barked, "Quick,

quick, slow, slow."

"This isn't so hard," Dev whispered in her ear.

"Like walking," she agreed, "only more fun." The tune playing overhead got to the chorus and half the line of dancers seemed to recognize the song at once, loudly echoing the famed line "All my exes live in Texas."

In only a short while, they'd fallen into a comfortable pace that felt as if they'd been dancing together for years, not less than an hour.

The music came to a stop and the tapping of the mic sounded overhead again. "Everyone stop and turn to face away from your partner."

Turning as directed, Angie found herself facing a total stranger, followed by the unexpected foul odor of stinky cheese.

"Now," the music started again, "let's see how much we've learned and make new friends."

The stranger introduced himself. "I'm Harvey." He waved this thumb over his shoulder. "Margaret behind me is my intended."

"How do you do. I'm Angela." She couldn't bring herself to encourage the misbelief that she and Dev were an item, and was thankful when the line of dancers began to move—until Harvey's palm slid slowly down her back and thick stubby fingers rested casually against her derriere. As casually as he had, she stretched her arm behind her and lifted his hand higher up her back.

"Did you try any of the hors d'oeuvres? The shrimp bruschetta is excellent." As if she hadn't just redirected his hand a moment before, Handsy Harvey dropped the same stubby fingers to her backside once again.

And once again she reached behind her and shoved his hand up her back and almost choked at another whiff of stink.

"My favorite were the bite-sized nachos. A little refried bean and cheese on a wafer."

And *that* explained the stinky smells.

"And turn again," the crewman called out without stopping the music.

Nothing was a more pleasant sight than Dev facing her with open arms. She curled against him, a little closer than she had previously, and gave thanks that the man didn't have an affinity toward refried beans. At least she didn't think so.

Before the end of the lesson, she'd had a quick turn with Dev's father, tripped over Handsy Harvey when he forgot which direction he was supposed to be going in and plowed into her and Dev's dad, and she learned to do turns while moving forward without stepping on Dev's foot.

"That was more fun than I'd expected." Angie followed the crowd out of the room.

"Especially when you stopped stepping on my feet." From behind her she could hear the smile in Dev's voice.

She slowed, and twisted part way around to see Dev better. "I only stepped on you twice."

"More than enough," he continued to tease.

"Ooh. Excuse me." Another passenger bumped into Dev, sending him tripping forward into Angie.

The two wobbled in place a moment, when Dev's hand brushed against her arm. "Are you all right?" He hovered nearby, his gaze steady on her.

"Me? Couldn't be better." If she'd been on this cruise dancing with this man in another time and for another reason, she might have been down right wonderful.

Outside the lounge, Julia and Dev's father were huddled with their new group of friends, chuckling, and of course, holding hands. Dev really wanted to be happy for them, really he did, but he was simply too practical to let the illusion of love at first sight trick his dad and Julia.

"There you are." Julia grinned at him. "Have I introduced you to Ben and Geri?

His surprise must have shown on his face because the woman who had flagged his dad and Julia down earlier this morning, stuck her hand out at him and chuckled. "Short for

Geraldine. Who knew I'd fall in love with a Benjamin."

"I bet you explain that a lot," Dev answered.

"We do."

Julia flashed a grateful smile at her friends. "They sail all the time and have been giving us lots of tips."

"I probably know these ships better than the crew." Geri swung around to face Angie. "Your mom has been telling us all about you but she didn't say what a wonderful dancer you are."

"Honestly," she waved a thumb over her shoulder at Dev, "he made it look easy."

"Well, you looked like you knew what you were doing. You make a very nice couple."

Angie shook her head. "Oh, we're not a couple. We just met."

"Really?" Something about the way Geri smiled put Angie on alert. "Anyhow, about lunch, I'm just sorry we didn't know you two would be on the ship. Yesterday before everyone else got hungry, we made reservations for lunch today at one of the specialty restaurants. When I called earlier this morning to add the two of you, the hostess said they were booked solid and didn't have a bigger table available."

"That's fine." Angie waved casually, reassuring her. "I don't eat much at lunchtime anyway."

Ben leaned around his fiancée. "I even tried to change it for another day, but this massive group has them all booked up. It's the most romantic restaurant on the ship. Good food, good music, good views, and of course," he paused to kiss Geri tenderly on the temple, "good company."

Geri giggled and swiped her hand at him. "You are so silly, but I love it."

"You don't mind, do you?" Julia asked her daughter. Dev didn't know her very well, but even he could see how torn she was between the lunch plans and her daughter.

"Of course not. I have some work to catch up on anyhow. You guys go and enjoy."

"Thank you." Julia pulled her grown-up little girl into a hug.

"If you have lunch in the restaurant, today is the day they have their fresh baked cranberry almond bread." Geri kissed her fingertips. "Unbelievably delicious. Sounds awful, but it's not. And they only serve it one day a week.

Ben tugged at Geri's elbow. "And our one lunch reservation for the week may pass us by if we don't get a move on it."

"Who needs a watch with this guy around," Geri teased. "We'll see you around."

On that note, the four wandered off and Angie turned around to face him. "I don't know about you, but if I don't sit down, I may fall down. Who knew all that two stepping could wear a girl out?"

Together they cut their way through the sporadic cluster of people and grabbing hold of her hand, he nudged her to follow him on deck. "This is closer than the buffet."

"Don't expect an argument from me. A comfortable lounger sounds great about now."

"Good." He picked out a spot on the far upper deck that most people overlooked and sat her near an umbrella. "Give me five and I'll be back with lunch."

"Oh." She swung her legs over the lounge chair and settled her hand, ready to stand up. "You don't have to bring me lunch."

He waved her down. "You're right, I do not *have* to do anything, but there's no reason for both of us to stand in line."

The corners of her mouth tilted up in that cute smile of hers. "What's for lunch?"

"Hot dogs sound okay?"

"With relish and mustard and lots of onions?"

"No sauerkraut?"

The smile slipped and her nose crinkled with distaste.

A contented laugh erupted. "A woman after my own heart."

"I wouldn't object to some sweet potato fries if they have them."

"Got it." He offered a one finger salute and hurried over to the lunch bar at the end of the adult pool. A few minutes later, tray in hand, he headed for the lounger.

One leg drawn up slightly, Angie rested an elbow on her knee while her hand shaded the sun from her eyes. A woman about their age seemed to be explaining something with considerable animation. But it wasn't the woman or her enthusiasm that had his undivided attention at the moment. Even though he'd spent the entire morning with Angie, not until this very minute had it struck him just how beautiful she was. There were professional models who couldn't strike such an appealing pose. And it didn't hurt any that with her knee pulled up, the shorts had ridden up her thigh and gave a splendid view of very shapely legs. Something deep inside told him the rest of this trip might be harder than he'd expected, and for totally different reasons than dealing with his dad.

CHAPTER TEN

"Oh, that does look delicious." The woman who had been talking at Angie without stopping for a breath waved at Dev. "I'm Renee. My cabin is in the same hall as Angie's."

"Yes," Angie twisted to face him, "we shared an elevator on my way to meet you for breakfast."

"I was telling her to hang on to you."

Dev blinked. "Excuse me?"

The man looked like an overgrown three year old trying not to show how completely confused he was. Casually placing her hand over her mouth, Angie hoped the woman didn't notice she was laughing.

"My husband and I have been married for almost ten years and if he brought me lunch on vacation, I'd probably faint from surprise. As a matter of fact," those animated hands started up, "I'm on my way to get *him* lunch. Not that I mind, but still…" She blew out a wistful sigh and waved a lazy thumb at Dev. "So hard to find men who really share all the work. I'm telling you, any man like this fellow who does is worth his weight in gold."

Dev cast a quick glance in Angie's direction, but if he wanted some direction he was out of luck.

Angie shrugged at him, then smiled up at the lady. "Thank you."

Letting her gaze roam appreciatively over Dev and the tray of food he held, her new friend blew out another sigh and eased back a step. "I'd better get moving before the ship runs out of food."

Angie had been spent enough time on a ship for the thought *Like that would ever happen* to pop into her head.

Dev nodded at Renee. "Nice to have met you." When the woman blended in with the cluster of passengers making their way through the deck area, he set the tray down beside Angie and sat across from her on the next chair. For a moment she thought he was going to say something, but instead he reached for his lunch.

Hot dog in hand, Angie took her first bite and a delighted moan slipped from her throat. "Oh wow. This is really good." She wiped a dab of mustard away from the corner of her mouth. "What did you get?"

"Pretty much the same concoction only mine has a dribble of ketchup too." He lifted the onion covered hot dog to his mouth and for a split section she thought she saw his eyes roll back in his head. "Oh, this *is* good!"

"Would I lie?" she teased, before taking another bite.

Hot dog halfway to his mouth for a second bite, he paused and softly chuckling, shook his head. "How would I know?"

"I'm telling you, I wouldn't. Now you know!" She reached for a French fry and taking a bite, bobbed her head. "Yep. This is definitely going to become a staple on this trip."

"Just what everyone comes on a cruise for. Fine hot dog dining."

It was nice to have someone to laugh and joke over lunch with. It hadn't really occurred to her just how lonesome being happily alone all the time could be. "You're not mocking an American tradition, are you?"

"Wouldn't dream of it."

She smiled back at him and practically inhaled another bite.

"So," Dev wiped a stray dab of ketchup from his chin, "any new thoughts on our parents?"

"They're stubborn."

He chuckled again. "I don't know about your mom, but that's nothing new for me."

Gripping the remainder of her hot dog, her hands lowered. "I didn't see your father do one thing that I could hold out as a red flag for their future."

"Ditto. Your mother seems like a very nice lady."

"That's because she is."

"Okay. So we agree they're nice people." Dev dunked a fry in the ketchup on his, plate. "But that doesn't mean they should be getting married."

"Not after only two weeks. When I think back to high school, it was Mom who always cautioned me on being careful. On never being sure of a person's true colors. Not to judge a book by its cover. Just because a guy was good looking or a star athlete didn't mean he was good boyfriend material. My sophomore year I dated a nice kid. Mom thought he was nice too, liked that he always rang the doorbell when he picked me up, always called her and dad sir and ma'am, always had me home on time, then after a couple of months he got caught with some of his buddies stealing bottles of scotch from the corner liquor store. Mom lectured me forever on a person's true colors. If I'd been the one to tell my mother I was marrying a man after knowing him only two weeks, she'd blow a gasket."

"Exactly." Dev waved the ketchup covered French fry. "My father would be the first to tell me that marriage is a lifetime commitment, and not something to be rushed into. He wouldn't care how old anyone is, or how well the couple know what they want in a mate, he'd remind anyone within earshot that the foundations for a solid relationship take time to grow. Period."

This whole thing created a constant churning in her stomach that had nothing to do with the greasy fried foods she'd just eaten. "We'll come up with something."

Angie's hall-mate came walking back in their direction. Arms laden with a loaded tray, she paused as she approached Angie. "How was it?"

"Delicious," she and Dev echoed.

"Good, because I got the same thing for us." She grinned and kept walking. Stopping just past where Angie sat, the woman leaned her head back. "We should try to get together for something. Maybe an after dinner drink here on the deck."

"Sure," Angie answered, more out of being polite than

out of interest.

"Wonderful." The woman took a step and paused again, glancing around her before leaning in low. "You're the nicest couple we've met so far."

"Well, that's sweet of you to say, but—"

"Really, I wouldn't have said it if I didn't mean it." She straightened to her full height. "I'd better get back before the fries get cold and soggy. We'll talk more later." With a slight bob of her head, the woman was off in search of her other half.

Shifting on her lounger, Angie looked up at Dev. "Guess there's no point in mentioning we're not a couple."

"We may have to give up on that one."

A crazy thought flipped a switch in her mind. "You know, that gives me an idea."

Dev reached for a pickle and set it back on the plate. "What gives you an idea?"

"That we're not really a couple."

Pickle dangling between his fingers, he kept his gaze on her.

"Don't say anything till I'm done."

He took a quick bite and nodded.

"What if we get married too?"

Dev blinked hard. The heat and sun had to be the reason why the woman he barely knew had just suggested marriage. Either she was suffering from sun stroke or the heat had affected his hearing.

"Don't look so stunned."

"How should I look? We've known each other less than twenty-four hours."

"That came out wrong."

His first thought was *that's a relief*, except oddly enough, it wasn't. The original declaration wasn't sitting poorly with him as it should.

"We both agree our parents would be appalled if we had

decided to marry all of a sudden to a person we barely knew."

He nodded. So far she made sense.

"So what if we gave them a taste of their own medicine? What if we wait another day or two, because we really don't have too much more time than that, and announce we have decided they're right? When you know you know, and we're going to have a double wedding."

He had to think about this for a minute. Normally he would've spouted something about her being completely out of her mind. At the moment though, he had to admit she might be onto something. "So in other words, if we can make them focus on why we have no business getting married, then hopefully that will make them see why they have no business getting married either. Am I following you?"

Grinning broadly, she practically bounced in her seat. "Yes! It's perfect. You know that it's human nature to want to do what people tell you that you cannot do, so we'd only be giving them reason to dig their heels in if we keep insisting they shouldn't marry. Even if they begin to have reservations, they may do it just to prove to us that they know what they're doing."

As much as it surprised him that he'd followed her convoluted trend of thought, he had to admit she did indeed have a point. "So we make nice for another day or so and then make the big announcement?"

She nodded.

"They'll never buy it." He shook his head.

"Sure they will. Would you have thought a month ago that your father would marry a woman he knew less than two weeks?"

He shook his head again.

"I rest my case. I think we can do this. Are you in?"

"I'm in." It was probably the best idea they'd come up with so far. Especially since reason wasn't working. "We'll have to do a little better planning than what we came on board with."

"Agreed." She put her hand over her eyes and glanced

up at the sky, then reached into her purse and pulled out a small bottle of sunscreen. "Do you have anything in mind?"

"My first thought is we need to cram a few months of courtship into the next twenty-four hours."

"That might be a little industrious."

"Think of it as cramming for a final exam, because you'd better believe if we put this out there, that we've discovered enough about each other to realize this is it, that you're the only one for me, they are going to drill us for all we're worth.

Rubbing lotion onto her face and neck, she stopped mid-stroke. "I hadn't thought of that."

"Here." He extended his hand in front of the sunscreen. "You missed a spot. Let me help."

Slowly she rolled her arm forward and uncurled her hand exposing the 100 SPF lotion. "I burn easily."

He should have realized that. Her skin was as close to porcelain as human flesh was possible. Blonde hair, blue eyes, and fair skin were the perfect recipe for sunburn. Rubbing the lotion between his hands to warm the liquid, carefully he rubbed the back of her shoulders, barely reaching under the edge of her sleeveless blouse. "I used to date a girl who was fair skinned like you. Her dad owned a boat so the family lived on the water all summer. There'd always be a streak of white against a strip of fire red skin where her fingers couldn't quite reach. This part of her shoulders and the top of her feet were the worst offenders."

Her gaze followed the slow movements of his fingers. "Not everyone is as careful as you." A halfhearted chuckle rumbled in her throat. "My best friend growing up would always slap it on thick and fast. Inevitably there'd be a red streak down the middle where she'd missed. One summer my back looked like a zebra for weeks."

Wiping his fingers dry along the back of her neck, he smiled and capped the bottle. "I bet you made a very pretty zebra."

"Don't look now, but my mother and your father are coming out of the solarium."

It took a second to recognize her mother. She had

donned a floppy pink hat that he had not seen before, and one that Angie could use. His father was right at her side, his hand at the small of her back, either gently guiding her through or protecting her from the flow of people, or both. Dev pushed to his feet, and extended his hand to Angie. "We might as well get this show started. Let's go for a walk, it will give us time to think and then something to talk about."

A bright smile took over her face. "Excellent idea."

Wrapping his fingers around hers, they made their way to the path that looped around the deck and hoped this excellent idea didn't turn out to be another massive mistake.

"Do you see them?" Julia Cannon stood at the edge of the pool holding her hat on her head and scanning the surrounding lounge chairs for her daughter. "Oh, look!"

Raymond followed the direction her free hand pointed to. "What am I looking at?"

"It's them." Arm straight out, pointer finger waving in the wind, she drew Ray's attention to their children. "And they're holding hands!"

"He probably doesn't want to lose her in the crowd. I wouldn't read too much into it if I were you." Ray kissed his fiancée on the cheek. "They're probably plotting to hogtie one of us, and Shanghai the other."

"Don't be ridiculous. I think they're starting to get used to the idea."

Grinning at her, Ray brushed the back of his finger along the edge of her jaw. "That's one of the many things I love about you. Always the optimist."

"Not so much when we decided to wait for the last minute possible to tell our kids our plans so they wouldn't try to stop us. It was a bit cowardly."

"That was being practical. Another thing I love about you. Besides, seeing as how my workaholic son dropped everything to follow us, it's a safe bet we were right. They just might have hogtied us until we came to our senses."

Julia smiled widely and kissed him square on the lips. "I love how you make the ordinary world with all its flaws and foibles, and stubborn children, a fun place to live. Something tells me we're in for one heckuva ride."

CHAPTER ELEVEN

Hands draped over the edge of the railing, the deep blue ocean shining brightly in front of him, Devon bit back a laugh. "That sounds like one heck of a trip."

"Despite the circumstances, I am expecting this one to be considerably less complicated."

Dev cocked his head sideways. She'd told him quite a bit about her friend Pam's wedding and divorce cruise, and yet there was no doubt in his mind that he had barely scratched the surface. "Ever been tempted to take a walk down the aisle yourself?"

She shook her head, but kept her gaze forward on the slightly rolling waves. Her head might be shaking no, but the distant look in her eyes told him there was a story there.

Another long moment of comfortable silence passed and he found himself answering his own question. "The girl with the porcelain skin, she wasn't just a girl I used to date. She's the only girl I've ever come even close to marrying."

Angie dragged her gaze over to him.

"We met the summer before my senior year at college." Even after all these years, he really hated retelling the story. So why was he telling her now? This wasn't a real engagement, a real relationship. But he wanted her to know nonetheless. "We stayed together after graduation and all through my MBA studies. Eventually, getting married seemed like the logical next step, but I just couldn't bring myself to pop the question. Then one day she ran off to Vegas with my best friend. They're still married. Have three kids."

"Sounds familiar," she huffed. "Do *you* want kids?"

"Some day." Not something he really thought about. At least not the way some of the women in his past seemed to have their futures planned out to the nanosecond, including kids, dogs, and summer homes. Only right now, at this moment… "Yes, I think I do."

"How many?"

He tipped his head in her direction and smiled. "Is this part of the final exam?"

Cheeks already flushed from the sun and wind, darkened in hue. "Just curious."

"I honestly don't know. What about you?"

"Four."

"That was fast."

She shrugged. "I'm an only child. I've always known I wanted children, as in more than one."

He could understand that. Many a time in his life he'd wished he had a brother, maybe even two.

"So it's a given I want at least two. If you stop at three, the middle one always winds up with some issue somewhere. But with four, you eliminate the middle child syndrome and all is well."

"Okay," he bit back a laugh, "can't argue with the psychology." For a split second, he had a vision of a living room very much like the one he'd grown up in. A large Christmas tree in the corner, and four kids shaking and unwrapping piles of packages in the middle of the room. The parents on the sofa, drinking hot cocoa and smiling, were a bit fuzzy, but he had a feeling he was the dad. Interestingly enough, the idea of four kids seemed a whole lot more appealing than it had even a few minutes ago.

Fingers linked, she leaned closer against the railing. "Thought I'd found the perfect match. I was a freshman in college. We dated for almost three years. Broke up a bit here and there, but always came back around. It was like a magnet and true north. I thought we belonged together."

Silence hung a long few minutes and he wondered if he should ask for the rest of the story or leave it be, but he could see the sense of loss in her eyes and he very much wanted to make it better. "What happened?" he ventured softly.

The short chuckle was more of a scoff. "I got scared."

"I find it hard to believe that the woman who took off halfway across the country on a moment's notice to save her mom from my terrible father, would scare easily."

"Ha. No. My heart wanted happily ever after but my head said we'd be miserable. That I'd never live up to the expectations he had."

"That bad?"

She nodded. "He treated me like a queen. It was wonderful. Always so respectful, so considerate. Then one day I realized it was more than that. To him, I was the perfect little woman on a very high pedestal who could do no wrong."

He winced. Healthy respect was one thing, but this sounded like much more.

"There was no way any mortal woman wouldn't some day come tumbling down off that pedestal and shatter into a million little pieces. So, we graduated and I broke it off. Haven't spoken to him since."

"Sounds like you did the right thing."

"That was so damn long ago, and yet, even after all these years, sometimes, like now, as I look out on the ocean and think always a bridesmaid never a bride. I try to picture my life when I'm old and toothless, and wonder if I made a mistake."

"For what it's worth, I don't think so."

Ever so slowly, she tore her gaze away from the water to look at him. The doubt so strong in her eyes that even he could see it. "Why do you say that?"

"I've seen a couple of marriages where the husband had what the professionals would call a Madonna complex when it came to his wife. It might have been good for a few years, but in the end, the wife was very unhappy."

Her head bobbed, and a weak smile appeared on her face. "And when I stop feeling sorry for myself, that's exactly what I tell myself. Thank you for reminding me."

"Any time." Clapping his hands together, he pushed off the rail and turned about. "So, here's the litany of fascinating information we've learned about each other.

Your favorite color is green, favorite pie blueberry—"

"Sour cream. Don't forget the sour cream, makes all the difference in the world with a blueberry pie."

"Imbedded in my memory banks for life," he teased, then continued. "You prefer ocean to mountain, and company to being alone."

Angie nodded.

"You value friends and family and will go out of the way for people you care about."

"I didn't say that."

"No, but your stories did. You also love your mother very, very much, and there's nothing you wouldn't do for her. Oh, and you have a weak spot for Heavenly Hazes."

"Ha." She barked out a laugh. "One trip to Santo Domingo. One mistake." Her words were scolding, but her tone was happy.

"You play a mean game of cards. If we ever play rummy I need to watch it, because you can count cards like the best of them, and if we ever go to Vegas I absolutely will be betting on you."

She laughed even louder this time. "I don't know about that last one, but my turn."

Arms crossed, he leaned back and waited.

"Favorite color is blue. Favorite food is lasagna. The reason you made the two step seem so easy is because your mother insisted you know how to dance and taught you."

"She made it fun."

"I remember. Like me, you bought your house early on your own as both an investment and retirement plan."

"Right on."

"You love a good bourbon once in a while, but you're really more of a beer and pretzels sort of guy."

"Something that doesn't bode well after thirty." He patted his still flat stomach and made a mental note to spend a bit more time in the gym this trip.

"You seem to be boding just fine to me." She giggled.

"I'll take that as a compliment."

Her expression softened. "As it was intended."

It felt perfectly natural to reach over and cover her hand with his. Maybe this upcoming charade would prove to be more easily convincing to his parents then they'd first thought. Maybe.

Angie glanced at her watch. She'd had no idea how the ship would pull off a cooking class in the middle of the salon, and even now she still didn't see it. Even though the event was actually open to the entire ship, the room was fairly empty. So far only four couples, including themselves.

"Yoo hoo." Her mom waved from the back of the room, and dragging Raymond in tow, trotted up to them. "Sorry we're late, we were looking for you after lunch."

"We were out on deck enjoying the lovely weather."

Raymond made a waving gesture with his hand. "I told you."

"Yes, dear. You did." The words came out more sweetly than Angie would have expected, and the accompanying smile was an equal surprise. Deep down she was delighted to see them so in tune, but the cynic in her wondered how long her mother would feel like smiling.

Thanks to the restrictions of a cruise ship and lack of sinks and stoves, the cooking class was for mealtime summer salads.

"No way a salad is a meal." Dev leaned into her, speaking from the corner of his mouth.

Doing the same, she whispered, "Who knew there were so many varieties of goat cheese on the ship."

For the next forty minutes they ripped lettuce, spinach, and greens that as far as she was concerned should have stayed in the fields. Every so often an errant leaf would go flying over a shoulder, or a bowl. Finally, out of sheer boredom, Dev began shooting baskets. The leaves his weapon of choice, her shirt the basket. Fortunately, he was a lousy shot. Except…

"Hey." As casually as she could, she swiped a finger at her cleavage in an effort to discard the wayward leaf, but no luck.

Grinning like the proverbial Cheshire cat, Dev blatantly stared at her cleavage. "Want me to try?"

Playfully, she smacked his hand and pretending to pay attention to the instructor on the stage, she shook her head. "I'll get it out later."

"Can't blame a man for trying." He bit back a smile and tossed a handful of Craisins into the bowl, and she had no idea why, but she knew what he was thinking of doing with the rest of the Craisins.

"Don't. You. Dare." Waving her finger, she did her best to look sternly at him.

Eyes wide with surprise, he slapped his open palm against his chest, feigning insult. "Moi? Would I do such a thing?"

"Yes." She bobbed her head sharply. "Keep your hands to yourself."

Trying really hard not to laugh too loudly and disturb those around her, somehow she and Dev still managed to produce a passable dinner salad. All in all, she'd never had so much fun *cooking*.

"Where to now?" he asked.

"Napkin folding," Julia announced pleasantly.

Dev's head snapped to his father, who merely smiled and shrugged.

Angie was pretty sure her expression matched his. "This should be…er… interesting."

As with the cooking class, it was the company that made for the event. She even laughed outright, regardless of who was watching, when he gave up on the swan and merely dropped the napkin on his head like a veil and holding another napkin fluffed like a bouquet, teased his dad about *getting married in the morning.*

Since the scrapbooking class, unlike the game time and dance lessons, was open to all passengers, the two of them opted to bow out and watch from the bar. Ben and Geri had joined their parents for this one. Angie didn't want to know where they'd been for the previous two couple's events.

"I bet people think our folks have been married for years," Dev said without taking his eyes off his father and her mother.

"They do look good together, don't they?"

He nodded.

Out of curiosity, she shifted her attention to her mom and Ray's new friends. "It's not just their age."

"What?" he turned to face her.

"Look at Ben and Geri, they're not as fluid. Don't move like they've been doing things together a long time."

His gaze returned to the scrapbookers and his dad's new friends. "No. I don't think they do."

The crew member in charge of the program thanked everyone for coming, mentioned the bingo game starting in the Lido lounge at the other side of the ship, and gathered up what was left of the supplies while a handful of passengers stopped to chat her up.

"What do you say?" Julia stood in front of them. "Bingo?"

"We have a set of free cards." Geri fanned out a stack of bingo cards and waved at herself, batting her eyes.

"Cute." Ben shook his head.

"Fastest way across the ship is through the casino."

"Oh." Angie sighed. "There's always so much smoke in there."

"Hold your nose." Her mother looped elbows with her and started walking. "Are you having fun?"

Much to her surprise, she actually was. "Yes."

"I see you and Devon are getting along well."

She almost voiced the objection that they weren't a couple and barely knew each other when it hit her that if she wanted her mother to believe she had fallen in love at first sight, she needed to get with the program. "Seems like a very nice man."

Her mother glanced over her shoulder and smiled at Ray walking several feet behind them with his son and their friends. "If there's any truth in the old adage the acorn doesn't fall far from the tree, then he's probably very nice."

Angie nodded at her mom and considered the last two days. If only there really were such a thing as everlasting love at first sight.

"Oh look." Her mother let go of her arm and rushed

ahead of her into the casino.

Not till her mother stopped in front of a pair of slot machines did she understand what she was supposed to be looking at. "What?"

"Vintage slot machines."

"Slot machines come in vintage?" For Angie, the word vintage always implied clothing, cars, or the inside of the house that somebody wanted to sell for more money than it was worth.

Her mom rolled her eyes at her. "You really need to get out more, dear. Nowadays slot machines have cards. They're cashless. The days of putting coins into a machine, pulling the arm, and having a river of coins come out when you hit the jackpot have been gone for years." Her mother caressed the machine gently, noticing a small printed notice to one side. "Oh, isn't this fun?"

"Isn't what fun?" Raymond sidled up beside her.

"Do you have any nickels?"

Raymond stuck his hand in his pocket and pulled out a few coins. "Only these. I don't need money on the ship."

"That'll do." Julia accepted the change gleefully, very slowly slid the coin into the slot, and then closing her eyes, smiled. "Here goes nothing." She pulled the long lever toward her and squealed like a teenager.

"I didn't know you liked the slot machines." Angie was starting to wonder just how well she really knew her mother.

"Oh, they're so much fun, but so dangerous. Last time I took a cruise with your father they still had these old machines. He'd give me a roll of nickels and I'd sit here and happily pull the lever all night while he played twenty-one or craps."

"Daddy played craps?"

Her mom stopped and stared at her. "Your grandmother taught him how to play cards the same as you, but he learned craps in the Marine Corps."

"Oh." Angie wasn't sure why it bothered her that she hadn't realized this about her dad. Pushing the odd feelings aside, she read the card that had made her mom so excited.

"The card says these old machines are being toured around the fleet. They'll be on each ship for a month before the machines are donated to the gambling museum in Monaco."

Julia put the last nickel in, took a deep breath, and pulled the lever. Everyone stood about staring at the spinning fruit. One by one the reels stopped, the first displaying grapes, the second lemon, and on down the row until the last reel stopped at a match of three of a kind. A small bell chimed and a slew of nickels poured onto the floor, her mother's hand cupped underneath, creating a cascade of silver. "Oh, I forgot how much fun this is."

"You hit the jackpot?" Angie couldn't believe her mother's luck.

"Heaven's no. If I hit the jackpot this machine would be making lots of noise and the coins would keep coming. This is just a little kiss."

Some kiss, Angie thought.

Hands firmly on her shoulders, Dev whispered into her ear. "Everything okay?"

She nodded, watching her mom scoop up the few remaining coins. All she could think is, who is this woman and what had she done with the real Julia Cannon?

CHAPTER TWELVE

A thin stream of sunshine shone through the gap in the window curtains. Not a lot of light, but enough to nudge Devon awake. Last night had lasted well into this morning. Once Dev's dad was able to drag Angie's mom away from the slot machines, the group had enjoyed a really nice evening together. First, dinner with Geri and Ben and another couple from the Destiny group. Then they'd moved on to one of the lounges for a very enthusiastic game of music trivia. Apparently, that was another thing his father and Angie's mom had in common. Somehow the two were able to pull titles of songs that had been hits ages before either was born. Though it hadn't hurt any that he and Angie, being the youngest of the team, created a balance for the newer songs. Since the previous night's escapades at karaoke had gone so well, the entire group of new friends had shown up for tonight's open mic. Only this time it was Angie and her mom who did the duet, a ripping rendition of the old song "King of the Road." Dev was surprised the ship had it available, but he supposed considering how many senior passengers they had onboard, it shouldn't be that odd to find a hit song from long before his time. As expected, Angie and her mom nailed it. Apparently in some things, the acorn really didn't fall far from the tree.

By the end of that lineup, most people headed to their rooms after what had already been a very long day. In an effort to make their plan more believable, after their parents announced they were turning in for the night, Dev and Angie made a show of staying up to go dancing with Renée and her husband. Fueled by caffeine and good music, they'd found themselves shutting the place down. All of which meant that rolling out of bed this morning after only a few hours sleep was not going so well. If not for the stupid reverse psychology plan they'd agreed to follow through on, he'd have begged off on today's itinerary and crawled deeper under the covers until lunchtime.

A rap on the door dragged him out of bed. Flinging the door open, he was ready to lambaste who ever had the audacity to invade his morning when a tall steaming to go mug of the ship's specialty coffee appeared under his nose.

"I thought you might need a little morning boost."

"If I weren't half dead and too stupid to fall over, I'd kiss you." He walked away from the door, taking a long slow swallow of the heavenly brew.

Angie stepped inside and closed the door behind her. "I noticed yesterday that you take your coffee with milk and sugar. I hope I got it right."

"Perfect. Thank you." He swallowed another rejuvenating sip and noticed she looked awfully bright-eyed and bushy tailed for someone who had gotten as little sleep as he had. And pretty too. "Were you able to reach your friend?"

Angie nodded. "First thing this morning. I wish you'd been there. At first Mina thought I was making the whole thing up. Having you there would have saved me about fifteen minutes of convincing. When she finally realized that Mom really had met a nice guy who had a son as upset about their plans as I was, she was flabbergasted. By the time I got to the part about what our next plan is, I had three sisters screeching in my ear to be careful."

"Really?" He took another long sip.

"Really." She flashed an embarrassed grin. "You'll be happy to know that according to Jo—who did the fastest internet check ever without telling me—that you and your father are squeaky clean and have passed the Ummarino screening."

Cup halfway to his lips he paused and looked up at her again. "The what?"

Shaking her head, Angie waved him off. "Never mind. Shall I text Mom and let her know to go ahead and start breakfast without us?"

He shook his head. "If you don't mind, have a seat and I'll be right out. I only need five minutes in the shower and I can be ready to go."

"That's because you don't have to dry your hair." She sat on the edge of the unmade bed, briefly debating if she should at least straighten the covers and quickly deciding it would make her look like a dork. And of all the looks she'd gone for this morning, dork was not one of them.

"No." He chuckled. "Can't say that I have that problem."

"Ship's been docked for almost an hour. Folks are lining up to go ashore. Hopefully the lines won't be as long by the time we need to leave or we may have to cut breakfast short."

Another rap on the door had them both turning.

"Are you expecting somebody?" Angie pushed to her feet.

"Nope."

"Then you go on and get in the shower. I'll take care of whoever's at the door."

Having flung the door open, Angie faced Dev's father standing in the hall, a tall cup of coffee in hand, and a blank expression on his face. "I thought Dev could use a little morning wake me up."

It took all she had not to stumble over her own words. Hopefully her cheeks weren't brightening the shade of ripe cherries. "He's in the shower, will be out in just another minute, and then we're going upstairs to meet you guys."

He handed her the coffee. "I'm sorry, I didn't anticipate bringing a second cup. But feel free to drink this one yourself and it will be our little secret."

A slip of a smile that lifted the corners of his face did little to calm Angie's embarrassment. Under the circumstances, she knew better than to try and explain or she'd wind up rambling like a guilty teenager. She settled for a simple, "Thank you."

As the door closed, she set the coffee down on the dressing table and decided that it was probably all for the best.

"Who was it?" The bathroom door opened and standing shirtless in a dark pair of shorts and rubbing his hair dry with a white towel, Dev looked like he belonged on the cover of a magazine. Or maybe a romance novel.

"Your dad." She grabbed the coffee and held it out to him. "He brought you this. He really is nice."

Dev nodded and looking at the cup, one eyebrow shot up high as his glance shifted to the closed cabin door. "Interesting."

"Why do you say that?"

"I don't ever remember my father bringing me a morning cup of coffee in bed, so to speak. I wonder what he's up to?"

"You think he's up to something?"

Dev nodded. "Maybe, but," he glanced at the clock on the wall, "we have plans of our own."

Yes, they did. And after chatting with the three Ummarino sisters, she had serious doubts about all of it.

"I knew it." Standing at the slot machine, Julia Cannon nodded at her fiancé, clutched a plastic coin-filled cup in one hand, and pulled the handle with the other.

"Yes," Ray stepped closer. "What I couldn't tell is how long she'd been there."

"What?" Julia paused her game and turned to him.

"For one thing, she was fully clothed and apparently waiting for him to get out of the shower."

"So?"

"How many women do you know who have to wait for men to get ready?"

Julia stiffened a moment, prepared to take offense, but the truth was, she really didn't know any women who had to wait for their husbands. She wasn't totally sure where human society had gone wrong. In the animal kingdom it's always the male of the species who has to be beautiful to attract the female. Why in heaven's name the human race got that backwards she didn't know. "Okay, maybe. What was the other thing?"

"Only one side of the bed looked slept in."

"Well, I did raise her right." Julia slipped another coin into the slot machine. "This is so pretty to watch. Even when it just sucks up my money and doesn't spit it back. I didn't appreciate how much fun these old machines were. The new ones just don't cut it. Don't have the same joie de vivre."

"The slot machines?"

"Yes. Pushing a big button isn't the same as pulling the lever, and putting a card into the slot once isn't as much fun as putting in coin after coin, and all the electronic sounds are fine, but none of it beats the cascading coins and trying to catch them in your cup. You should try it."

Ray chuckled. "I think you're having enough fun for the both of us."

"If you say so." She dropped another coin in and pulled the handle.

"What I say is, we should get moving if we're going to meet the kids for breakfast."

Julia gave a wistful sigh and patted the machine. "Stay full for me. I'll be back tonight."

"Good thing we won't have one of those in our home."

"Maybe." Julia smiled wide, and dumping the coins into her purse, looped her arm in his, kissed his cheek, and grinned. "Or maybe not."

"You are going to love the barbecue lunch they do on the island." Hefting the beach bag higher on her shoulder, Angie scanned the docking area.

"I am?" For Dev it seemed almost surreal how comfortably they had fallen into their roles.

"I think so. I mean, I do. If you like barbecue it's absolutely the best. Unless. If you don't like barbecue. Do you? I mean…"

"Relax." Smiling, Dev reached for her hand ready to pull her in closer and at the last second settled for squeezing her hand with a quick shake and letting go. "I love barbecue."

"I thought so."

"You did?"

"Well. I guess from watching you the last few days, it seemed to me you would love it."

"You're right." Again, less than twenty four hours since deciding to put on a performance for their parents and already they could read each other better than any relationship in his past, including his ex with three kids.

"There's our guide." Ray pointed to the man to the far right of the gangway, waving a small sign with the excursion name on it.

"I've always wanted to ride in a glass bottom boat." Julia rubbed her hands together enthusiastically. "What better way to start the day is there?"

"Under the water," Angie deadpanned.

"Don't remind me." Julia shuddered. "I can live with snorkeling but scuba diving seems so risky."

Dev smiled at the nervous mother. "It's not if you follow the rules. Besides, they don't go very far off shore or very deep here. This is geared more for folks who learned to dive in the ship's pool. We'll be fine."

The group of tourists from the ship, including Ben and Geri, boarded the small bus that took them across the private island to a different pier. A few of the experienced divers had brought their own gear, but most were vacation divers like Angie and himself. He'd been so surprised to learn that even though she had only dived that one time on her friend's wedding cruise, she'd loved it and was eager to do it again. For some reason he'd pegged her as a quiet, risk adverse, sweet girl next door. From her diet colas to her blushing nature, she fit the bill to a T. But there was a flip side, a bold, fearless side that included belting out a song in front of strangers, winning at poker, dancing up a storm, and now scuba diving.

"I'm entrusting you to keep my little girl safe." Julia

held his gaze.

"Mother," Angie groaned, enunciating every syllable very clearly.

Dev tried not to laugh at the mother daughter interaction. Not wanting to tick off either member of the duo, he held the mother's gaze and nodded. A silent agreement made; he had the strangest feeling that his assurance went much farther than just scuba diving, and Julia was the first to know it.

His dad and the others going for the boat ride were directed along the pier to a typical tourist boat, a small portion of the group were escorted to the other side of the scuba hut where snorkeling gear, boogie boards, and ordinary floats awaited along with a thatched roof bar that promised hours of tropical refreshments.

"I'm Jeff," the man on the scuba boat introduced himself. "Who has your own gear?"

Several hands shot up.

"Great. Follow Ricky here." He pointed to the young kid next to him. "The rest of you follow me and we'll get you all set up."

Another thirty or forty minutes and the scuba passengers were suited up and properly briefed on safety procedures and what to expect. The expectation portion of the little speech had Dev smiling so hard his face felt like it might crack open. The little boy in him hoped to see at least a small reef shark. There were a few lakes near his hometown where he and some friends would go diving every once in a blue moon, but it had been years since he'd gone anywhere with fish the color of rainbows and the promise of corals and honest to goodness shipwreck debris with clear visibility well past his nose.

Angie leaned into him. "Are you as excited as I am?"

"Depends how excited you are. But yeah, I'm pretty stoked."

Every diver paired off, completed their buddy check, and one hand across their middle, the other holding their masks, one by one, each strode into the ocean. Angie, then Dev, were the last two off the boat. Swimming within an arm's length, Dev led the way.

The scuba shop near the pier had the option to rent the little GoPro camera. After only a few minutes under water, Dev was glad he hadn't second guessed himself and passed. He didn't have a clue which of his friends would tolerate being bored by reefs that resembled anything from a green cactus to a Spanish flamingo dancer's fan, but he took the photos anyhow. They were almost at the end of their first allotted time when Angie spotted the sunken boat reef they'd been told about. Even from a distance it was fascinating.

Already Dev made a mental note to come straight back for their second dive and do some serious exploring. Hurrying ahead of him, Angie slowed at the arrival of a school of parrot fish and somehow jarred the snorkel loose from her mask band. Not an uncommon occurrence for a diver to lose the unused piece of equipment, he anticipated her descent to retrieve it, Dev kicked a little harder and shifted his direction. He didn't like having her too far ahead.

The snorkel landed softly on the sandy ocean floor only moments before Angie caught up to it. Her arm extended, she latched on. At the same moment she gave him a thumbs up with the other hand, her snorkel wasn't the only thing that lifted. Raising the snorkel from the ocean floor, the sand beneath it shifted and what must have been an unhappy awakened stingray sprang upward.

Angie's arms flew up, propelling her body to tumble backwards, leaving her feet up. Scissoring at the water more forcefully, Dev could see her hesitation in righting herself, feeling instant relief when she found her bearings and turning toward him, gave him another thumbs up. He hated to point out that their time was up, but she beat him to it, tapping at her wrist. With a nod, he waited a few seconds for her to reach him and slowly they began their assent to the surface.

Able to see their boat a little ahead, Dev glanced down at his gauges when a gray shadow swam past. Turning to get a better look at the departing fish, the touch of something against his arm had him whipping his head back around. Stiff as a board, staring straight ahead, Angie had reached out and latched onto him. She'd seen it too.

Wrapping his fingers around her forearm, he swam with her the short distance. She was the first to break the surface and he came up still holding her hand. Pushing his mask above his head, he spit out his mouthpiece. "You okay?"

Angie nodded, then immediately shook her head, then nodded again.

Instinct kicked in and he pulled her into the fold of his arms. Eyes closed, mask still on, mouthpiece out, she leaned against him.

"Was it the shark?"

Her head bobbed.

"It was just a little one." He brushed his hand along her exposed jaw.

Still resting against him, she shook her head. "Didn't feel that little when he brushed past me."

"Come on. Let's get on the boat."

He could feel her drawing up the energy to swim a couple of feet and climb up the ladder. Once onboard, they'd stripped out of their equipment, dropped their masks in the water tubs, and when it was just the two of them standing side by side, he dared ask again. "Better now?"

She drew in a long breath and nodding, blew it out slowly. "The stingray just surprised me, but the shark scared the crap out of me. By the way, did you get a picture of either?"

He shook his head. "I was otherwise preoccupied."

"Too bad. Now that my heart rate is back to normal, swimming with sharks is going to make great dinner conversation."

For half a second, he thought she was going to smile.

"It's silly," she continued, "but I don't think I really grasped how common sharks are in these waters until he swam up to me slow enough to think he might be considering having me for lunch."

"At only about four feet, he's probably still a baby. He's not ready for big people food."

The joke fell flat as Angie slowly leveled her gaze with

his. She was definitely not amused.

"I'm sorry. Come here." This time he didn't talk himself out of what came naturally. Taking a step toward her, he tugged her against him and wrapped both arms around her tightly. "Can I get you something? Juice? Water?"

Her head moved from side to side and she loosened her hold around his waist. "I'm okay now. Really, I am."

When she drew back far enough for her face to be within inches of his, he almost forgot they were on a public boat with plenty of people milling about, and almost did what came very naturally. Blast all these people.

CHAPTER THIRTEEN

"We saved you a seat." Julia waved her arm over the table. "And there's a dish of ribs and some corn to start, if you'd like."

"Thanks, Mom." Angie slid into the empty bench across from her mother. She had a feeling that by morning she would be hearing from muscles she didn't even know she had.

A rib halfway to her mouth, Angie's mom stopped and set it back on the plate. "You look a little peaked. Feeling all right?"

Angie reached for a plate. "A little sore. I don't use my swimming muscles every day."

Julia looked from her daughter to Dev, waited a moment, then looked back. "Did you swallow water?"

"No." Somehow she felt rather foolish having been so spooked by a common Caribbean reef shark. Several of the people on the boat had encountered him or a sibling and all were as excited as a kid in a candy shop. She was the only one who had almost had a heart attack.

"Angela Elizabeth Cannon."

"No. I didn't swallow water." Angie almost made light of it a second time, but knowing that hiding from her mom hadn't worked in all her years, there was no point in evading her now. "I just got spooked by a shark."

"A shark!" Her mother slapped both hands against her chest with the drama of an elderly southern Baptist clutching her pearls.

"It was just a baby," Dev interjected. "A harmless reef shark swimming by."

"Harmless?" her mom repeated.

"If I hadn't been startled by the stingray, I might not have been caught so off guard when the shark appeared. We *had* been told they're common in these waters."

"And you got in the water anyway?" Her mother was not handling the news well.

"Mom. It's not a big deal. I admit my life flashed before me, but Dev was right there at my side and a half dozen other divers weren't far off. We were all perfectly safe."

Dev curled his fingers around her hand closest to him and squeezed. He'd done that several times today and she was not only getting used to it, she was beginning to like it.

Interestingly enough, at the same time that Dev had reached over to offer his support, his father had done the same thing, silently reassuring her mother. This entire trip was very much the most surreal experience Angie had ever had. One crazy thing atop another, one surprise atop another, and she wasn't sure she was ready for whatever unexpected thing the universe had in store for her next.

On deck after a hurried shower and change of clothes into his tuxedo, Dev had no idea why people called cruises restful and relaxing. So far, he'd had more steps in his day than a marathon runner, and the formal night schedule was equally packed. "I don't care what's on the schedule. Tomorrow I'm going to relax in the sun and enjoy the ocean breeze for at least a little while."

"Sounds fair enough." In a stunning, form fitting deep pink gown that showed off a guitar-like figure, Angie stood at his side and leaned over the railing. "Truthfully, I wouldn't mind a break either."

"So, are you ready to go do this?"

"No."

That wasn't what he'd expected to hear. Especially since this upcoming charade was the only plan they had.

"I don't mean I've changed my mind. I still think this is our best bet at making them rethink their decision. But you may have noticed earlier today, I have a hard time keeping secrets from my mother. I'm not all that sure I can pull this off."

"It's up to you. I'm willing to come up with a new plan. I'm even willing to lock Dad in the closet on the wedding day if it comes to that." Realizing how that sounded, he held up his hand. "Not that I don't think your mom is a nice lady. I even think they get along extremely well. For all I know, this thing between them could work, but any rational human being would back us up in suggesting they wait to make sure."

Angie straightened her spine and lifted her chin. "You're right. This is for her own good. I owe it to her."

"Do we have our story straight?" He moved in a bit closer.

"After spending a few days together, we've discovered how much we have in common."

He nodded. "How being together, spending time with each other, just feels right."

"And thanks to Mr. Shark," she sprouted an amused smile, "I realized life is too short to play it safe all the time."

"Yes." He brushed the back of his hand across her cheek. "We'll repeat what your mom said—when you know, you know."

"Know. Yes," she uttered softly.

If there was ever a time to take a chance, tonight— now—was it. Sliding his fingers behind her neck, he came in even closer and let his lips settle on hers.

The gentle, tender, and bone-melting kiss was exactly what she remembered. If she was going to play at this game, she might as well go all in. Arms around his neck, she pushed up on the tips of her toes and let the rest of the world fall away. Staying here like this for the rest of her life seemed like the best idea she'd ever had. But this wasn't her reality.

Letting her arms slide down to her side, she took a step back.

"We, uh, should be, er, comfortable with each other. That is, if we want our parents to believe us." Dev's fingers slid down her arms and linked with hers.

Hands resting on his lapel, she nodded but her mouth had gone totally dry, words weren't coming.

"Dad and Julia's Destiny cocktail gathering should be over by now."

"Yes. We should go find them."

"We'll have to start playing nice." He smiled. "Nicer."

"Nicer," she repeated.

Letting go of one hand and tightening his hold on the other, he turned them away from the rail and began walking along the deck. "We're off to see the Wizard."

There were many things to like about Devon Miller, but easily making her smile or laugh had to be at the top of the list. "To the Wizards."

They'd made it all the way to the sliding doors when coming from the opposite direction, arm in arm and dressed to the nines, their parents strolled up.

"We were just taking advantage of the lovely moon before going inside to meet you." Her mother didn't bother separating from her fiancé.

Angie, on the other hand, quickly pulled her hand away from Dev's hold. Mostly a knee jerk reaction to being caught with a boy by your mother, but until they set the game in motion, she wasn't totally comfortable.

"Out on the quiet seas, on a moonlit night, is the perfect setting to clear your thoughts," Dev addressed his dad.

"Absolutely. No better place to escape the world."

"Why don't we find someplace quiet to have a little chat?" Dev gestured to the door with one hand, and reached for Angie's hand once again with the other.

"Not sure there is such a place as a quiet corner on this ship." Raymond led the way.

"There's a nice spot outside the pizza parlor." Dev followed Angie inside, still holding her hand.

"Pizza?" Julia frowned. "I'm not exactly dressed for pizza."

"They also serve specialty coffees and teas. We can have a cup at a table and avoid the crowds till our dinner seating."

"Now that sounds like a plan. Then I can hit my slot machine if it's not taken."

Ray shook his head. "You do have a one-track mind."

"I'm not the only one who appreciates the older machines. Most of the time I've come around looking, someone is parked on it and won't leave."

"Gives us more time to enjoy the trip." Ray smiled at her and the sweet way her mother looked over at him made Angie want to smile too. She really did hope if these two married some day that whatever it was they had between them would stay as sweet.

The walk up to the pizza deck was a short one. Her mom got her traditional French roast, as did Ray. Angie was about to order her usual diet cola when Dev surprised her by ordering a hot tea and she decided that was a much better idea.

"So." Dev settled into the small table in the back corner of the deck. Holding Angie's hand, he dropped the entwined fists on his leg. "We've done a lot of thinking about your wedding plans."

"Look, son. We've been over this already."

Lips pressed tightly, Julia leaned forward and stared at her daughter. "At our age it doesn't take long to—"

"Yes, Mom," Angie cut her off. "We know."

"If you two would give us a minute." Dev waited for both parents to nod before continuing. "We've given a lot of thought to what you have to say. We've also had an excellent opportunity to spend quite a bit of time together these last few days and have discovered that Angie and I have a great deal in common—besides the two of you, that is." He chuckled. "We enjoy the same pastimes, the same music, have similar senses of humor, have a healthy respect for family—even when they're behaving foolishly. But more importantly, working insane hours and being driven by my career, I didn't realize how much I was giving up. After spending these few days not just existing, but really living life *with* Angie, I can't see myself going back to working alone nonstop."

Angie's heart did a little quick step. How amazing would it be to have a man say something like that about her and really mean it?

"As you have pointed out," Dev continued, "even at our age we've been around the block enough times, dated enough people, to know the kind of person we would like to spend the rest of our life with. You are absolutely right, I won't think Angie is anymore perfect for me next week, next month, or next year, than I do today."

At the same time she felt her heart squeeze, she heard her mother's surprised intake of breath, noticed her wide eyes and hand over her mouth. Part of Angie wished that all of this was real. That she and Dev truly were in love with each other, but another part of her felt a wave of optimism at her mom's reaction. At least something good should come from Dev's amazing performance. Would the man ever cease to surprise her? She really could love this man so very easily.

Dev squeezed her hand and she realized he was cueing her for some input. "I couldn't have said it any better myself." She looked to him and smiling as sweetly as she could, reminded herself that the look in Dev's eyes wasn't love but good acting. Then letting all the emotions running around inside her show on her face, she prayed her mother interpreted it as true love.

"So," Dev looked away from her and faced their parents again, "we'd like to join the Destiny group and get married with everyone else."

Silence hung and Angie was ready to do a foot-stomping cheer. She just knew their parents were searching for the right words to tell them they were both crazy.

"You want to get married now?" Dev's dad asked.

Both of them nodded, but Dev answered his father. "It's like you've both said over and over, why wait?"

Ray and Julia looked at each other and Angie was positive they were having a silent conversation with their eyes. When the two gave a half nod in agreement, Angie wondered how the heck had they mastered that so early in the relationship.

Angie's mom whipped around, clapped her hands together, then sprang out of her seat, ran around the small table and hugged her daughter so tightly, Angie wasn't sure she could catch her breath. "I knew it!"

"Scoosmee," Angie muttered still squished in the bosom of her mother's embrace.

Her mom leaned back, Angie's face held between her hands. "It was the shark, wasn't it?" Julia turned to Dev. "Staring your mortality in the face has a way of making you see life more clearly." She turned back, kissed her daughter on the cheek and on a huge sigh, sat back down next to her fiancé. "You're going to be so happy!"

"What did we get wrong?" Angie stared at her diet cola. After commemorative formal portraits, a lobster dinner, and bubbling good wishes, it was decided the brave decision required a toast.

So, now they were all at the Champagne bar listening to a band in tuxedos play tunes that Dev hadn't heard since he was a kid watching the oldies movie channel with his mom. Dev took a sip of his drink.

"Do you think they just need time to let it sink in? To see that this is nuts?"

"I honestly don't know, but what I do know is that we're going to have to ride this charade out."

Angie nodded. "Agreed. So for the duration, we're now in love and can't live without each other."

"Yep. That about covers it."

Her gaze on their parents dancing, her eyes seemed almost sad.

"Hey." Dev took hold of her hand. "Is it your mother or something else?"

Angie chuckled. "Developing those fiancée mind reading skills?"

"Maybe." He shrugged with a smile and holding her hand, tugged her to her feet. "Tell me about it on the dance floor."

It took a second to recognize the old tune. Something by Cole Porter or maybe Gershwin. On a night when they were all dolled up in black tie attire, the music seemed a fitting homage to an era long gone by. As a kid he'd never paid a lot of attention to the song lyrics in the old movies. He wasn't even too sure who the leads were, but tonight he noticed the words. Whoever wrote them had to have been in love at the time or remembered every minute of falling for someone special. With every line, Dev found himself relating to the love struck singer. He was never going to forget tonight, this trip, or Angie. Not the way her eyes lit up when she smiled, or how she felt in his arms dancing all night, how she sang very much on key, and did indeed haunt his dreams, and beyond any doubt, changed his life.

"Have I mentioned how handsome you look in a tuxedo?"

He shook his head.

"How about how much I love the way you dance?"

"No." Was it crazy that his heart skipped when the word "love" came out of her mouth? Just to see her smile, he twirled her in place and then curled her back into his arms. Delighted when she leaned in closer. It seemed only appropriate that the next song was about dancing cheek to cheek.

"May I cut in?" Julia tapped on Dev's shoulder.

His dad smiled at Angie. "Likewise, if you don't mind."

"Not at all." Angie smiled back and curled away from him and into his father's hold.

"You two make a lovely couple." Julia waited patiently for Dev to move his feet.

Standing with more personal space between them, Dev moved across the floor with Angie's mother much the way he would have with his own mom.

"I admit I didn't expect you to see the connection this quickly."

"Connection?"

"From the first day I saw you two together. There was that look in your eyes when your gazes locked. It was solid, respectful, and just a little awed. The perfect foundation for a lifetime together."

"You saw all that standing in the karaoke lounge?"

"Well. Maybe not the first, first time. I was pretty angry with her and didn't see much past my own nose. It was the next morning at the breakfast buffet. I could see more clearly then."

Dev nodded, not quite sure what to say to that one. Not quite sure what to say or do about any of this, other than understanding the next few days could very likely be the best of his life, and his undoing.

CHAPTER FOURTEEN

"This is amazing." Using Dev as a chair, his arms loosely around her waist, Angie took another lick of the homemade coconut dream ice cream.

Dev leaned around her, tugging at the arm holding the cone. "You're supposed to share."

"I am. One lick for you," she held it out within his reach, "and two for me."

"Hey." Dev laughed that deep rumble that made her heart warm.

"No fighting over the ice cream." Julia waved a finger at them.

Geri stuck a spoon in her cup of mango mix. "Let the kids have fun. You're only engaged once and they only have a few days left."

So far they had spent the last two days gallivanting from island to island, seeing every tourist sight available, and then participating in every evening game show the ship provided. All along the way playing up the lovey dovey engaged couple for anyone watching.

The scary part for Angie was that playing the part had become easier with every stop. And with every new thing they'd shared, she'd almost forgotten they were acting at all.

"So, according to this," Ben turned the walking tour map of the island he held in his hands, "next stop is the old churchyard. The tombstones date back to the 1500s."

Geri looked less than thrilled. "That's actually a stop? Looking at graves?"

Ben shrugged.

"Oh, come on." Julia hopped up from her seat, tossing

her napkin in the trash. "Reading old tombstones can be fun."

Sometimes Angie wondered about her mother's perspective on fun.

Holding hands, the three couples strolled the short distance down the two lane main drag that was more dirt than street. A little shop with a pink awning caught Angie's eye and she pulled Dev to a stop.

"What's this?" He peered over her shoulder into the window.

"It looks like a shell shop." Fascinated by the display of different size and colored seashells on display, she spun around to face him, not letting go of his hand. "Can we go inside?"

"Sure." Dev called out to the others that they would catch up in a minute and followed her into the shop.

"Oh, it's a souvenir shop." From the display of shells, she hadn't expected the diversity of goods in the store.

Dev turned over a mug to look at the bottom, set it back down, then reached for a wooden statuette on a different shelf, also turned it over to look at the bottom before setting it back down. "This isn't just a souvenir shop, it looks like it's an artisan shop. Everything appears to be handmade, and from the looks of it, possibly one-of-a-kind."

Still holding his hand, they slowly inched their way from case to case, closely looking at each display of goods. One souvenir plate in particular caught her eye. She'd debated where would she hang the sunrise on porcelain if she bought it when she noticed Dev admiring a shelf loaded with hand-blown glass. "Oh, my."

"Yeah. That's what I was thinking. This dolphin is amazing."

The sea mammal stood about five or 6 inches tall and no matter which way you turned it, the dolphin's eyes seemed to follow you. Not in a creepy horror movie way, but in a sweet, don't you want to be my friend way. From some angles you could see multiple shades of blue and green and clear crystal, and from other angles just a stunning shade of Caribbean blue. "I can't imagine how hard it would be to make something like this from scratch."

"Agreed. I have many skills, but no talents."

"That's not true." She whirled around, standing chest to chest, smiling up at him. "I happen to know you are a fantastic dancer."

"That's a skill." He leaned forward and kissed her nose. "But thank you."

"No, it's not. I mean, yes, it is a learned skill, but to be really good, there has to be natural talent. Lot's of people take lessons and still look like a robot on the dance floor."

Chuckling softly, he shook his head ever so slightly and slid his arm around her waist. "Has anyone ever told you that you have a way of making people feel special, and every day worth looking forward to?"

Surprised at the sweet compliment, she smiled and shrugged. "Can't say that I have."

"You, my dear lady, are a gem." Leaning closer for what she thought was going to be another quick peck on her nose, his lips landed briefly on hers, leaving them tingling and wanting more. "Let's pay the man for the dolphin and find our parents."

"Mom's going to want to stop in here after she'd done reading tombstones."

Dev laughed again. "Your mother really is something else, isn't she?"

"Honestly, I haven't seen this fun-loving side of her in a long time, but I think I can get used to it."

"So could I. And I think my dad already is."

"Hey, are you two planning on buying out the store?" His dad stuck his head inside and waved them forward. "Stop with the doe eyes. We need backup or your mom is going to stick with the tombstones the way she's attached to those slot machines."

"Yes, sir." Dev saluted his dad, paid for the dolphin, and not through the entire process of wrapping and giving change did he ever let go of her hand.

Yep, maybe they both had embraced their roles a little more than they should have.

This whole remembering that loving Angie was just an act was becoming harder and harder for Dev. With every passing day, doing things together, laughing together, seemed so natural that everything he'd said to their parents had come true. He'd truly had fun discovering new things about her. Angie made it easy to see how life with the right person could make living one ordinary day at a time an adventure. He couldn't imagine going back to his sedentary life without her in it.

"Yoo hoo." Renee waved at them from the top of the gangway. "Did you have a good day?"

"A blast," Angie called back.

"Did you try that little ice cream shop?" Renee sidled up beside her new friend once Angie reached the ship's deck.

Angie nodded. "To die for."

"Which flavor did you have?"

"Coconut dream."

"I had the Guava. Who knew guava could taste so good." She turned to Dev. "And you?"

"We shared." He waved a thumb at Angie and then raised his brows at her. "Sort of."

"Hey, two for one. Known balance for sharing." She grinned up at him. The way she played along with his teasing was another example of making an ordinary ice cream cone an adventure to have fun with over and over.

"Absolutely," Renee concurred. "Handsome and I are having dinner at the steakhouse tonight. We tried to snag a reservation for four but couldn't pull it off."

"No problem. We're stuffed anyhow. We were just discussing skipping the main dining room and grabbing a bite in the buffet after we shower and change. Oh, I need to show you the coolest glass dolphin we bought!"

"From the shell shop?" Renee practically bounced out of her shoes.

"Yes!" Angie squealed.

"We bought a turtle, but it took forever to decide. I really wanted to just buy it all."

"We felt the same way."

The casual way she used the word we about them made the corners of his lips tip up.

"Sorry to break this fan fest up." Renee's husband tugged at his wife's hand. "But we have a dinner reservation."

"Catch up with you later," Renee said. "After the show."

"All right." Angie waved and faced Dev. "All that talking about steak dinners and I might be more hungry than I thought."

"I was just thinking the same thing. What do you say we cut across the promenade and grab a snack from the café?"

"I think that will just hit the spot."

Along the way to the café they'd paused long enough to watch a cake making demo in the center atrium. Some poor woman from the surrounding passengers had been roped into joining the captain and the chef for the demonstration. By the time they'd added whipped cream and cherries and chocolate layers to the German Chocolate cake, Angie's stomach was rumbling loudly. "I know how this is going to end. Now I'm really starved."

Dev reached for her hand and they walked a bit more quickly than usual to the café.

Seated in the only free table at the front of the open air area, Angie bit into the Italian hero sandwich. "Okay, what does it say about me if my favorite two foods on this ship are the hot dogs and the heroes?"

"That you're a woman after my own heart?" he teased. "What about the lobster?"

She wiped a drop of mayo from the corner of her mouth and swayed slightly side to side in exaggerated vacillation. "All right. The lobster was my favorite, but the hot dogs and heroes are close runners up."

Dev let out a loud chuckle and before they could finish their impromptu dinner, her mom appeared out of nowhere, his dad at her mother's side.

Julia held up a huge bottle of champagne. "Look what we just won! Did one of those silly raffles by the wine shop and we won!"

"Oh, how nice." Angie shot her mom a thumbs up. The woman had always been lucky with raffles and lotteries. Never the really big ones that made you a millionaire overnight, but Angie didn't think her mother had ever purchased a dud of a scratch off.

Dev's dad pointed to the bottle. "We thought we'd save this bottle for the wedding toast. It will bring all of us luck the rest of our lives."

Her mom took a step back. "I'm going to drop it off in my room and then we're off to dinner. Meet you at music trivia."

"See you then," Dev answered as they walked away.

"The rest of our lives," she repeated.

At her side, Dev nodded.

Angie set the remainder of her sandwich on the plate. "This plan is not working, is it?"

"It's a safe bet that our parents have no intention of delaying their wedding."

"We're running out of time," he stated the obvious.

"So, what do we do now?"

"I honestly don't know." And wasn't that the truth. Right about now, he didn't have a clue about an awful lot.

CHAPTER FIFTEEN

Angie had been right. The idea of their parents coming around to seeing the folly of a whirlwind courtship had not worked. If he was honest with himself, Dev had had little faith in the plan from the beginning but nonetheless had enjoyed every minute of it.

Even last night, after the dinnertime revelation, they continued the charade that for him was no longer an act. They held hands, he'd rubbed her shoulders when she stretched, and she'd patted his leg when he'd made a good guess. They'd laughed, teased, and the kiss goodnight at her door had lasted a fraction longer than it had the night before, which had been longer than the night before that.

Like it or not, they were going to have to have a heart to heart talk about how he really felt, if only he wasn't too damn scared that it might be the last talk they had as soul mates and the beginning of tedious conversations as step siblings.

"You look awfully serious. Coffee cold?" His dad took a seat beside him.

"No, contemplating the immortality of the crab." He looked at his watch. "Angie saved us lounge chairs in the sun. I was getting one last cup."

"You two work well together."

"Yeah, we do." He looked over his dad's shoulder in the direction of the coffee station he'd come from. He was used to always seeing his dad and Angie's mom at each other's side. "Where's Julia?"

"We had breakfast earlier. She's gone to stake her claim to the slot machine. I don't expect to see her for a while."

"She really is enjoying that thing. Do you think she's

developing a problem?"

"With gambling?" His dad shook his head. "No, she's just having fun with it. It's hard to lose much money with nickel slots, and I think some of it is just the rare opportunity to relive something she enjoyed a very long time ago."

"If you're sure."

His father nodded. "Very sure."

"I thought that's what you would say." Dev pushed his chair away from the table. "I wish the two of you this happiness for the rest of your lives."

"That means a lot to me. To us. More than you can imagine." His dad slapped him on the back of his shoulder. "Now, about you and Angie."

The ship's whistle broke the peaceful lull of a lazy afternoon in the sun.

"Wonder what that's all about?" Angie didn't bother opening her eyes. It was the first day she'd finally got to enjoy the sun and fresh air without having to be somewhere or do something.

"Last ship I was on, that blasted whistle went off every day with one medical call after another. It's amazing how many people trip and sprain something or just plain collapse from the heat." Renee looked around. "Wonder what's taking so long to mix up one little old Heavenly Haze." She placed her hand on Angie's arm. "You were so right about those things. Dee-licious."

"Just be careful. They pack quite a wallop."

The whistle sounded once again.

"And here we go." Renee huffed, scrunching her face and mimicking, "Alpha, alpha, alpha."

Except the loudspeaker voice repeated, "Bravo, bravo, bravo."

Renee's eyes popped open. "That's a new one."

Dev's gaze drifted around. "It's a fire."

"A fire?" Renee squealed, snapping upright.

"I do hope it's nothing serious." Angie looked around for any signs of real trouble.

"Here you go, ma'am." A broad shouldered bartender with eyes as blue as the ocean and a smile that made a woman's mind wander places it had no business going, flashed a wide smile and held out the tray for Renee.

"Thank you," Renee practically drooled.

"Enjoy." The good-looking guy turned on his heels.

Her gaze still lingering on the man's departing back, Renee blew out a soft sigh, "If only."

"Oh, my. Look at that!" A few chairs over, a woman with a huge floppy hat waved her fingers in her husband's sleeping face with one hand and pointed in the distance with the other. "That doesn't look good."

A plume of dark gray smoke drifted upward from the front of the ship.

Once again, "Bravo, bravo, bravo" bellowed from the overhead speakers. This time the voice sent the fire crew to a different location than before. At least she thought it was different. "That woman is right. This doesn't sound good."

"The crew knows what they're doing." Dev's calm words didn't match the sharp look in his eyes as he scanned the deck and horizon.

It occurred to Angie if something were seriously wrong, if they were in trouble, the crew would be around to deal with the people, but there wasn't a crewman in sight. Not even a bartender. Except for the woman still pointing at the smoke, most of the people outside seemed unconcerned with the situation. Heck, most of the people still soaking up the sun didn't seem to notice there was a growing situation. A couple strolled past them, holding hands, chatting softly, oblivious to the smoke, the whistles, or the handful of folks like herself watching with interest. "I can't decide if I'm crazy for wanting to know why there's smoke coming from below deck, or if all these people are insane for preferring sunbathing over safety."

Renee smiled at Angie before taking another sip from the fruity drink. "Small fires must happen on these ships more often than any of us would know. I'm sure the crew will take care of it quickly."

"I have heard stories." Angie nodded, putting her concerns in check. "My friend Michelle enjoys cruising and she had me rolling in laughter over a story while standing at the buffet when an electrical fire started. Lots of commotion, but in the end, no big deal." That little memory made her feel quite a bit better. Dev and Renee were right. The ship's crew knew what they were doing. "I'm not wearing my watch. How much longer till we're supposed to meet up with Mom and Ray?"

"Thirty minutes at the Champagne lounge."

"Ooh. I love champagne." On her second Heavenly Haze, Renee's already good mood was improving with every sip.

"Not sure why they call it that, but Mom really likes the music they play. She says it reminds her of growing up and the songs her mom liked to listen to."

Dev looked at the darkening smoke and sliding his hand around her shoulder, pulled her closer, and kissed her temple. "I think it would be a good idea to head downstairs a little early. Maybe find our folks."

Renee's husband nodded. "That sounds like an excellent idea. Come on, Renee."

"But I just got my drink."

Steve extended his hand to his wife. "Honey, there's more where that came from. We really should beat the crowds."

"Beat the crowds?" Renee clutched her drink more tightly. "You go ahead. I'll wait for you here."

"Renee," he said more sternly.

Several short blasts of the ship's horn sounded, followed by one very long blast.

"So much for beating the crowds," Dev muttered.

"Isn't that…?" Angie wasn't the only one unsure if the change in blasts was indeed an emergency signal. A few of the people who had been lying back, ignoring everything around them, sat up straight. Others who had been strolling stopped and looked up as if the sky would have answers printed in the clouds.

"Come on." Dev grabbed a tight hold on her elbow and nudged her forward. "We can find your mom and my dad on our way to your room."

"Let's go, Renee." Steve urged his wife to move quickly.

"I'm not leaving my drink." On her feet, she threw her cover up over one arm and carried her drink in the other.

Angie almost stumbled to a stop, making a conscious effort to force her feet to move forward and keep pace with Dev.

The same multiple blasts followed by one long steady blast sounded again. The sound of the speakers clicking on preceded the captain's voice, "All crew and staff to their assigned stations." He repeated the instruction one more time before the speakers clicked off.

"Not good," Steve muttered.

"Agreed." Dev picked up his pace.

"Will you people slow down," Renee fussed.

Once again the siren sounded, only this time the captain urged all passengers to report to their muster stations. The casual indifference shared by the passengers disappeared. With the exception of one woman slathered in tanning oil who merely turned the page on her paperback, the people lying on lounge chairs sprang up like a shepherd dog on alert for a fox. A few, carefully gathered their belongings into bags, or flung them over their arms while others already on their feet with their wares clutched to their chests, looked ready to bolt if only they had an idea of which way they should go.

"This is definitely not good." Dev scanned left then right and pivoted her around. "Looks like we might get below faster this way."

A flash of orange sparked to the side and a starting gun at a race couldn't have done a better job at sending people scurrying away. The people who had been casually strolling from one end of the ship to the other, picked up the pace as though rushing to catch a departing train at Grand Central Terminal. Kids were having the time of their lives racing past them, laughing and screeching. A perspective not shared by the people leapfrogging over the abandoned loungers in an effort to hit the hallways first.

The strength of Dev's arm pulled her more tightly against his side. "This isn't going to be as easy as I'd like."

At the doorway inside, the same guy who had served Renee her drink now donned a life jacket and pointed to the glass in her hand. "I'm sorry, ma'am, but no food or beverages at muster."

"I'll just wait here for y'all." Renee pivoted in the direction they'd just come.

"Renee, this isn't a drill," her husband reminded her.

"Okay. Fine."

Where Angie expected her new friend to put the drink down or hand it off, instead she kicked her head back and downed the entire thing in one very long swallow.

"This could get interesting," Dev whispered in her ear.

"I'm afraid so."

Compared to the near chaos on deck, inside the ship seemed much more orderly. Considering the captain had ordered all passengers to their muster stations, which meant first they had to go to their cabins to retrieve their life jackets, most people appeared to be milling about as if this were just another drill.

"I want to stop at my mother's cabin." Angie leaned into him but kept her eyes forward. "I know we're not supposed to, but…"

"I know. Let's see how it goes." Dev wanted very much to give Angie what she wanted, but he knew how quickly this situation could turn. Even though she and her mom coincidentally shared the same floor, they were on opposite ends of the ship. As with any fire situation, elevators were blocked. The designated crew waved all passengers toward the staircases. Packed tighter than a can of sardines, moving the passengers down the stairwell was a very slow process.

Hitting both rooms might be pushing their luck.

By the time they reached Julia and Ray's floor a hint of smoky aroma teased at Dev's nostrils, and strobe lights were flashing in the halls.

"Disco," hands up in the air, Renee shook her shoulders and sing songed, "where the happy people go."

Somehow Dev had missed when the woman who had downed her drink in a single gulp had slipped her shoes off, and now had one dangling from one hand, and in rhythm to her shimmying shoulders, twirled the other shoe from her other hand. Too bad there was no time to stop for coffee.

"Here we are." Angie slowed as they approached her mother's door. "Oh, it's open."

Dev reached the door a moment before she did and nudged the solid surface open all the way. The small room matched almost every other cabin on the ship. Except other passengers in their cabins were hurriedly banging doors, bumping into each other, retrieving the life jackets from the closet, and rushing back to the main stairways.

"Oh, dear." Angie straightened. "What…?"

From where he stood, all Dev could see was a man's rear end in dark shorts, white socks and sandals, with his head stuffed under the bed.

"Ooh. Party games!" Renee squealed, peeking over Dev's shoulder, then her brows dipped and her mouth twisted into the perfect pout. "What game is that?"

"Never mind, dear." Renee's husband, tugged his wife away from the doorway. "We'll get our jackets and meet you guys back on deck."

Dev nodded and returned his attention to the man squirming on the ground. Angie had nailed it. "What the hell?"

A strong thud followed by "ouch" sounded seconds before Ray Miller scooted out from halfway under the bed, rubbing the back of his head with one hand and dragging a couple of orange life jackets out with the other. "Has anyone ever told you that your mother is one stubborn lady?"

Obviously he was talking to Angie. At least, Dev

thought so.

His dad pushed to his feet. "Julia wanted more closet space so she put the jackets under the bed."

"That explains why you were under the bed." Angie nodded. "But what about my mother?"

"You mean where, not what. I can't get her away from the slot machine."

"What?" Angie flung her gaze from Ray back to Dev as if he had any answers.

"She thinks it's nothing serious and will be over before we get the jackets."

"That's insane." Angie blew out a deep sigh.

"That about covers it." Ray nodded, walking past them. "Maybe you can explain it to her."

Static sounded overhead and the captain made a muffled announcement. Between the commotion in the hall and the alarms in the background, it was hard as hell to understand.

"What did he say?" Ray stared up at the speaker in the ceiling.

Dev sighed. "They're lowering the lifeboats."

CHAPTER SIXTEEN

"**B**last that woman." Two jackets in hand and concerned etched deeply on his face, Ray Miller stormed past his son.

"Hang on, Dad." Dev cuffed his father's elbow. "Let's all go. Give us one second to get our life jackets. We have to walk past our rooms anyhow to get to the casino end of the ship."

His dad nodded and Angie cast a worried look in Dev's direction.

"It will be fine. Your mom is probably right. This will most likely all be taken care of and over before we make it to muster."

"I sure hope so." Angie followed him out the cabin door. "I wasn't too nervous before, but suddenly there's a knot in the pit of my stomach and I don't like it."

Neither did he.

The crew were scattered in every exit, encouraging the passengers to report to their emergency muster stations, hurrying the ones along who were still lingering in the hall retrieving their vests. Parents chased children down the hall, other children seemed to be running loose and free of adult supervision. Dev didn't get that at all. Once at their cabins, they were able to run in and out with the vests in a hurry.

They'd made it out the hall and up the first few flights. He'd anticipated more resistance from the staff but the throngs of people, though moving steadily, created its own chaos. A few people worming their way up the stairs instead of down went completely unnoticed.

"And there she is."

"Oh, Mother."

"Hi dear." Julia was still popping coins into the machine and happily pulling the lever as if the ship weren't on fire. Movie producers couldn't make this stuff up. All they needed was a band playing in the background.

"Where is the staff?" Dev didn't understand how anyone had left her here playing the slots.

"They're gone."

"And they left you here?" his father asked astounded.

"Not exactly." Julia dropped another coin in. "I hid in the corner until they'd done a pass through. Not very thorough, if I do say so myself. Had they tried, they should have seen me." She pulled again.

Ray handed her the jacket. "Put this on."

"This monster hasn't spit out one plug nickel all morning. I just know it's going to pay out big any minute. Think of all the things we could do with the money from a jackpot."

"Julia," Ray enunciated more deeply and sternly.

"Here." She handed her daughter the coins. "You keep putting it in while I put on the jacket."

"Julia!" Ray repeated more loudly.

"I'm putting it on."

Angie stared down at the almost empty cup of coins and up at Dev. He hadn't a clue what to say.

"Don't dilly dally," Julia urged her daughter, sliding the orange vest over her head.

Angie slid a coin in, pulled the handle, and shrugged when nothing happened. Before her mother could say a word, she stuck another coin in and pulled again. "This is kind of fun."

"Not you too?" Ray threw his hands up in the air and turned to his fiancée. "Let's go, we'll finish strapping you in on deck."

"Oh, one more second won't hurt." Julia had the audacity to look up at Dev and wink. As if he had anything to do with this insanity.

Angie pulled the lever. Not a single match appeared in the bars and Ray grabbed Angie by one hand and Julia by the other. "I'll cut you a check for the jackpot when this is over, but we are leaving *now*."

"Don't be silly." Julia sighed, reluctantly hurrying alongside Ray. "You don't have that kind of money to toss around."

When Ray didn't say another word, Julia turned to study her fiancé. "Oh, dear heavens. You do!"

Orderly chaos. That was the only way Angie could describe the crowds on deck. Ray had been right, several of the lifeboats were already in the water. The reality of abandoning ship hit her hard.

Dev placed his hand on the small of her back. The gesture, most likely intended to keep her close and safe, succeeded in squelching the panic that had threatened to rise up like Mount Vesuvius. "Thank you," she muttered.

"You were starting to look a little green."

"I'm okay. We'll be okay."

"Yes, we will."

Another few seconds and each passenger held their keycards under a portable scanner held by a staff member. Made sense. No time to search lists to check off names. Not until now had she realized that these weren't the lifeboats of old with people hanging over the sides, desperate for water and waiting to be spotted. For starters, they were covered and had a single narrow doorway on either side. No dying of sunstroke or washing overboard. On the inside, the boats held more people than Angie expected. Double rows and tiers fitted seats and people together like a jigsaw puzzle.

Her mom and Ray were helped on to the not so small boat and the crewman turned, reaching for her hand, and held the other up to Dev. "Sorry. Last passenger. You'll have to move over to the next boat."

Dev took a step back and Angie swiveled in place, reaching for the rope at the open doorway. "I'll get on the next boat too."

"No." Dev raised a hand to her. "Go. I'll see you soon.

It will be okay."

"I—"

"Stay with Pop and your mom." He backed away.

She didn't like it one bit. A crewman sat at the opposite open doorway, instructing and reassuring passengers that she'd done this a hundred times in drills and it's a piece of cake. In front of her, the crewman who looked more than a little relieved that he didn't have to wrestle her to stay in the boat, hooked the rope across the doorway and took a seat. All passengers secured and packed like sardines in a can, the lifeboat began its slow descent to the water.

All the while, Angie did her best to keep her eyes on where she thought Dev would be, seeking out a sandy haired head in a white shirt with neon turquoise shorts. The lifeboat still perched at the side of the deck blocked her view. Only the jostling of her boat as it hit the water managed to pull her gaze away for a few seconds. The passengers on board burst into applause, much the way she'd seen people do on an airplane. Personally, she didn't think there would be much worth applauding until they were all back on board a safe ship or on terra firma.

"That wasn't as bad as I expected." Ray smiled at her. She hadn't noticed till now how much the father and son looked alike when they smiled.

Equipped with a motor, something else all the old sinking ship movies hadn't prepared her for, the boat soared forward. With all the other lifeboats doing the same, they dipped up and over on what had now become choppy seas until stopping at what must have been considered a safe distance to watch and wait. Only she was less concerned with the mother ship and focusing on one little lifeboat. Just as had happened with their boat, Dev's boat began the painstakingly slow decent from the upper deck. Unlike their descent, halfway down, Dev's boat slowed and shimmied. Her heart gave a small stutter and she said a prayer of thanks that hers hadn't done the same or she might have lost the last thread on her panic control.

The little lifeboat kicked into gear again, lowering itself another level of windows when even from this distance she could hear a low squeaking sound that must have been loud as hell to those close up. The squeak was nothing compared to the pop as the rigging snapped and the left side of the dangling lifeboat banged into the ship.

"Oh, no," Julia muttered, accompanied by an echo of gasps and cries from fellow passengers.

All air had seized in her throat. She risked closing her eyes for a moment and saying a fast prayer. Eyes open now, she focused on the descending boat once again. She didn't have to be an engineer to know if their landing had been a bit bumpy, Dev's was going to be a doozy. "Come on, Dev. Just a little further." Somehow his boat seemed to be descending even more slowly than before. Concern for their own safety forgotten, all eyes remained glued on the dangling lifeboat. Voices around her murmured prayers and worries. Her fingers curled into a fist as she waited. Just a few more feet and the sound she never wanted to hear again ricocheted through the air. The other rigging snapped and the boat dropped rapidly the remaining distance, slamming into the choppy waters.

Julia's hand reached over to her daughter's, curling around the clenched fist. "Just a bumpy ride," she said softly.

Beside her mother, Ray spoke a little more firmly. "Bumps and bruises at best."

All she wanted was for the motor to start up and the boat to get close enough to see Dev's bumps and bruises for herself.

Her mother's gasp rang in her ear seconds before passengers began talking all at once and pointing at the bouncing lifeboat, listing to one side.

"What are they doing?" someone snapped. "Crazy people."

Another person muttered, "Boat must be taking on water."

Like ants escaping a knocked over hill, people poured out of the topside doorway. Backs pressed against the bright yellow sides, the passengers inched away on the tiny ledge.

"Oh, hell." This had to be a nightmare. Things like this

simply didn't happen in the real world.

"Look." Someone pointed to the back side of the cruise ship.

From the large doorway they'd used to enter from port, a massive rubber raft, more like what she'd expected when she thought of lifeboats, raced with two crew at the helm to the damaged boat. A small sense of relief wasn't enough to unclench her fists. Returning her gaze to the seriously listing lifeboat, she scanned the people still balancing along the small lip or climbing up onto the top. No sign of Dev. Finally, she spotted the neon shorts and breathed freely again. *Or not.*

Off to the side, a woman gripped something on the exterior wall of the small boat with one hand and held onto a small child with the other. The life rafts weren't close enough yet to render aid when an ear-piercing scream shattered the already tense air around them. The child had slipped from her grasp and fallen into the rough waters. And the turquoise neon shorts shucked the orange life jacket, diving in after him.

"It will be all right." Ray assured, "he's a good swimmer. Lifeguard all through college. It will be all right. You'll see." She wasn't sure if the repeated words were for her benefit or his.

"The water is so rough," she uttered. Seconds ticked by, maybe minutes. All sense of time melted into the fear. Where was he? It shouldn't take this long. "I don't see them."

Her mom's hand squeezed hers. "Have a little faith."

She said another prayer as a crewman with a safety rope around his waist dove in after them. "He should have had a rope too."

"There was no time," her mom whispered.

Ray repeated softly, "He's a good swimmer."

"There!" a voice behind them shouted and Angie snapped her head around to see where the woman was pointing at the same moment the boat erupted with another round of applause.

Bobbing in the water, she could barely see a sandy

haired head handing off a small child to one of the crew in the rubber raft. "Thank heaven."

"Seriously." Shaking his head, Ray Miller followed his fiancée. "The boat almost sinks and my son almost drowns and all you can think about is the slot machine?"

"It's not all I can think about. The fire is out and the ship is functioning well enough to get us to the nearest port. All passengers are safely back on board. Devon is dry and dealing with his admirers. The cruise line is flying everyone home who wants to go, or paying for anyone who prefers a stay at a lovely hotel for the duration of the trip, and either way all passengers will be offered a free future cruise for having to cut this one short. You and I have already decided what we're going to do. What else is there to do until we dock?"

They'd turned the corner and Julia came to a screeching halt. Ray almost bumped into her. "What?"

Perched on the red vinyl stool, a woman older than dirt dropped a coin in the same machine Julia had been nursing all morning, and pulled the handle. Each roll spun in the row. They waited and watched. One stopped, then another. From this distance, it was impossible to see the outcome, but the sirens and bells going off followed by the clanging sounds of cascading coins, they didn't need to see, they knew.

Julia sighed. "Told you it was getting ready to payoff."

"I'm sorry." Ray squeezed her hand.

"It's okay. I had fun. That's what matters." She turned to him, smiled, and gave him a peck on the cheek. "Besides, I bet that old lady doesn't have anyone to cut her a check."

Ray pulled her into his arms for a sound kiss unsuitable for public. "I do love you, woman."

"I know. Fortunately for you, I love you more."

"Doubt that."

"The response is, I love you best." Dev came to a stop

beside his dad.

Angie shook her head. "Don't start that or we'll be here all night as they out-love each other."

"Not possible," Ray said with a smile.

Julia beamed at him. "No. Not possible."

"I thought I'd find all of you here." Geri came rushing up behind them, Ben in tow. "What an exciting day."

"I could do with a little less excitement." Dev chuckled.

"You're a hero," Geri said with a bit more reverence in her tone.

"Thank you," Ray teased, and Julia shook her head.

Dev merely smiled at his dad before responding. "I didn't do anything anyone else wouldn't do."

"Don't fool yourself. Mother Nature scares the heck out of the best of us. Those were some pretty rough seas. I don't know about you, but I think a drink is in order." Geri turned away from the casino. "Last one to the Champagne Bar is a rotten egg."

The group pivoted and followed after Ben and Geri, but Angie hesitated and pulled Dev aside into the small cove outside the casino. "If everyone on the ship feels the same as Geri, this may be the most private moment we'll have."

Dev's gut clenched, his mind moving forward to all the unpleasant possibilities including there was no point in continuing the farce, while the rational side of him said no woman about to cut you off at the knees greets you with a stuffing-popping hug and kiss when she first sees you. "What's on your mind?"

"This." She leaned up on her tippy toes, wrapped her arms around his neck, and kissed him ever so gently. Leaving her arms loosely around his neck, she leaned back, still in his personal space. "These past days have been good."

He nodded.

Her eyes searched his. "Very good. Very possibly the happiest days since I was kid anticipating Christmas morning."

He nodded again, a smile threatening to cover his face. This didn't sound anything like a Dear John speech.

"I probably know you better than any man I have ever known."

"Ditto."

She put her fingers on his lips. "And love you even more. I didn't want to think about going home to my world the way it was, but thinking I could have really lost you forever made me understand what my mother has been saying. When you find what's right, life is too precious to waste time. I love you, Devon Miller, and want to see where this can go if we really give it a shot."

His hands locked around her waist, he pulled her in just a little closer. "Then I suppose it's lucky for us our parents were right about when you know you know, because I was thinking the same thing. I love you, Angela Cannon."

"Then we're going to give us a real shot?"

He didn't bother answering with words, instead he leaned in and kissed her soundly one more time before leaning back to go join others. "Ready?"

"After today? For anything. I can already tell, life with you is going to be one hell of an adventure!"

EPILOGUE

"This shouldn't be that hard a decision." Hand on her hips, Pam stood in Angie's room tapping her foot.

"Give the kid a break." Sitting on the edge of the bed, Michelle looked at the closed bathroom door.

"It's not like this is her wedding dress. It's just a little family party."

"Quit your fussing." Angie closed the bathroom door behind her. "How does this look?"

"As beautiful as the three before." Michelle smiled.

Angie turned to face the mirror. "Maybe I should try the yellow on again."

"No," Pam shook her head, "it doesn't matter what you wear. Devon will only have eyes for you. Trust me."

"I'm going to agree with Pam. Doesn't matter which dress you pick, you look fabulous."

There was no way Angie was going to tell her friends that she'd spent the last two days debating between slacks and a skirt. Not until this morning had she decided a pre-wedding party called for a dress of some sort. It was almost a miracle that she'd managed to narrow her choices to only three by the time Pam and Michelle came by to meet her.

The doorbell rang and Angie almost jumped out of her shoes. "Maybe I should try the pink on again."

Pam and Michelle moved to flank her on either side.

"You look beautiful," Michelle reassured.

Pam nodded. "That's probably Devon. Let's not keep him waiting."

"No." Angie sighed. The way the butterflies were flapping their wings in her stomach, anyone would think this was her wedding day and not the night before party. "Let's go."

From the bottom step, she could see her friends' husbands chatting with Devon and those butterflies did a nosedive. When he turned and smiled at her, the butterflies finally settled down.

"You look beautiful," he said.

Behind her, Pam muttered "see" as Michelle whispered "told you so."

"Thank you." Her gaze locked with his.

Dev stretched his arm out and slid her hand into his. "Ready?"

Something in the way he looked at her told her that he wasn't just asking about this evening's party. "Absolutely," she easily slipped her hand in his.

They were across the threshold on the porch when she heard Pam saying quietly behind her, "Guess that's our cue to follow. Last one out, lock the door."

Devon chuckled. "We probably should have waited and let them leave first."

"Maybe."

His hand lifted hers across his chest, tugging her in closer. "I'll confess I'm in a hurry to get through tonight and meet you in church tomorrow."

Leaning slightly against him as they walked, she glanced up at him. "That makes two of us."

"Did I ever tell you how much I love it when you lean against me?"

She shook her head. He'd never said as much but his tendency to always touch her in some way, to always respond warmly, told her more than words. "Better get used to it. I plan on leaning on you for a long time to come."

"Then I suppose it's a good thing I plan on being here for even longer."

"I think this is the best idea ever." Jo Ummarino pulled

another bottle of champagne from the fridge. "Society has so outgrown men sowing their final oats."

"Final oats sounds like an ingredient in a cookie recipe." Ginnie, the middle sister, tossed a bowl of her Aunt Maria's popular salad.

"That's only because you have a sweet tooth." Mina pilfered an olive from her sister. "Normal people would think of something like horses."

Angie, already holding a bottle of champagne in each arm, shook her head at her friends and neighbors. "That's why bachelorette parties are now common in our society. Not the cookies or horses part."

"Yeah," Jo agreed, "but this idea is way better. I just love a last night party. Not a bachelor or bachelorette, and no debauchery or travel expenses. Just friends and family from near and far gathering before the big day."

"The tradition has been in Mom's family for generations." Angie took a step back. "Since Mom and Raymond took advantage of the cruise line paying for a beachfront hotel to take their honeymoon, Dev and I were the only two people at the sunset wedding. This party is sort of celebrating all of us."

Jo shook her head. "I don't get why you and Dev didn't go ahead and get married in the Caribbean and take a paid-for honeymoon too."

"We considered it, but decided we'd rather celebrate with our friends and take the free cruise for our honeymoon."

"And fortunately for you," Mina smiled brightly, "you have friends who can pull off a wedding weekend with fantastic Italian food in only three weeks."

Ginnie looked up from the salad bowl in front of her. "Yeah, and if we hadn't had to wait for Ray and Julia to get home, we could have done it in two."

Handing her sister a bottle of their mama's home made dressing, Jo smiled at Angie. "It is nice that Dev will be moving in with you here and we won't be losing you as a neighbor."

"I think so too. It made sense since my house has the

space for two offices and an extra bathroom. Though the real deal clincher was when the house across the street went up for sale and Mom and Raymond snatched it up."

Ginnie's nose crinkled in confusion. "I thought I heard Dev mention they were buying over in Highland Park."

"No." Angie shook her head. "That was his father's idea. Mom almost had a cow when he suggested it. Never mind that it's clear on the other side of the next county over. Same thing with the ring he bought her. While Mom loved the idea that he cared more for her than his money, she insisted she'd break a wrist wearing that thing. She was very happy with matching wedding bands they picked up at a small shop on the island where they got married."

"That doesn't surprise me." Ginnie covered the salad. "Your mom has always struck me as practical with a sentimental streak, and absolutely no concerns about flashy appearances."

"Me too." Mina set four large loaves of Italian bread on the table. "I guess this means Pam's husband won't have to do your Christmas lights anymore."

Angie stopped and looked at her friend. "I guess not. Hadn't thought about it. I'll have to let Gil know he's off the hook now."

"I have a feeling he's already figured that out." Mina pulled a large bread knife out of the drawer. "And you won't be needing Uncle Tony's family discount anymore. Dev can probably fix all your little household repairs."

"Hold on. I know Dev is good at a lot of things," she raised her hand and bit back a smile, "but don't get ahead of yourself. Christmas lights are one thing. Plumbing is another. I think I'll keep my honorary member of the family card."

All the women laughed. Mina was really pleased to be keeping Angie as a neighbor, especially since they all got along well with Dev too. And who knew, maybe some day soon Mina could play aunt to some little ones.

Arms loaded with dry goods, Mina's mother closed the basement door behind her. "And what is the bride doing in my kitchen?"

Mina shook her head and sighed. "It's my kitchen, Mama."

"Tomorrow it's your kitchen. Today it's mine and your aunt Regina's and no place for the bridal party." Mama Ummarino shooed the girls out the back door.

Angie paused to kiss the blustery woman on the cheek. "Thank you, Mama."

The neighborhood example of motherhood who treated all the girls like her own, smiled and blushed. "You're welcome. Now go. And someone tell cousin Rosa that the timer went off on her lasagna."

Champagne bottles in hand, Angie stepped off the back porch and scanned the distance. "I still can't believe all this is happening. Just over a month ago I was worrying about broken water heaters and saving enough money to handle the next emergency on my own, and now I'm marrying the perfect man."

"The perfect man for you, yes," Mina corrected. "Devon is nice, but his name doesn't translate into Italian. My family would never forgive me."

The three sisters burst out laughing. The ridiculous idea sounded funny to anyone, but to them it was the degree of truth that made it downright hilarious.

"There you are." Adoration in his eyes, Dev greeted Angie at the bottom of the porch steps with a sweet kiss. "Thought you might have changed your mind."

Smiling up at him, the bride to be shook her head. "Not a chance."

Dev's arm looped around Angie's waist, joining them at the hip, something that everyone had gotten used to since she arrived home from her trip with a fiancé. The two wandered over to the makeshift bar to deliver the bottle of champagne.

"I don't care if his name isn't Italian. If anyone ever looks at me like that all the time, he could be green with a Mars return address and I wouldn't care." Jo leaned against the railing.

"I know what you mean." From where Mina stood, Angie had caught the brass ring. The woman had it all: a career, a home, and the proverbial good man. Mina's mom would kill to say the same about her daughters. Yes, they had a home, though it was shared between the three; and yes, they all had good careers; but for an Italian mother, that good man was key.

Most days Mina didn't care about the good man. She had a good life and was happy. Then there were days like tonight. Angie and Devon looked so darn happy. Any minute now Mina expected them to turn around and walk hand in hand six feet off the ground. The day the engaged couple walked into Mina's living room, she knew this was no ordinary man.

Not only had Angie been beaming from ear to ear, not only were they holding hands like a couple of smitten teens, but every few words that came out of Angie's mouth, Devon glanced down at her with such adoration it reminded Mina of a dog at the window watching his owner come up the front walk. Sheer, unconditional love.

"She does that a lot, doesn't she?" Jo stood next to her sister.

"Who does what?"

"Angie. She leans against him. Not in an I'm-going-to-fall-help-me way, but it in a way that shows she's always in tune to where Dev is. I kind of like the underlying significance."

"There's underlying significance to a lean?"

"Yeah. Every time she does it, he lifts a hand and brushes it against her arm. It's like they're always there for each other. Always will have each other's back. Kind of romantic."

Mina glanced at the two, who had now moved across the yard and were talking with Pam and her husband and the woman, Michelle, who had sold them the house and her husband. Mina thought it was nice how even though Michelle had moved all the way to California, married and had a child, she and Angie had stayed close. The three women seemed so different and yet anyone watching them laugh and chat could see they were definitely close friends.

"Didn't our seller meet her husband on a cruise too?"

Mina nodded.

"We should go on one."

"What?" Mina turned to her youngest sister.

"All three of those guys are smitten with their ladies. And Angie's friends have been married for years. I want one of those."

Mina shrugged. "Men can be difficult."

"They say that about us." Jo glanced at the friendly crowd in the backyard. "You know, Mars and Venus."

Someone turned on the music and Dev and Angie turned into each other and began swaying softly. A few more minutes and her friends joined her, and by the end of the song, half the party was following their example.

That was something she wouldn't mind—someone to dance with. Her dad was a wonderful dancer who taught his daughters early on to follow a strong lead. Too bad most of the men she'd known in her life hadn't had as good a teacher.

The screen door slammed shut behind her and her mom came out the door carrying a large bread basket in each arm. "Where is your cousin Rosa?"

"Oops." Jo hurried across the yard.

Mina's mom shook her head. "For a girl who is so smart, sometimes I wonder why her head doesn't just roll off her shoulders."

"Let me help." Mina reached for one of the baskets.

"The food is almost ready. We can start setting up the tables. Is everything ready?" Her mother glanced around the yard and smiled. "A nice party for a nice girl."

"Yes," Mina agreed.

"They are going to last, those two." Her mother lifted her chin in Angie's direction. She and Dev were now showing a handful of folks how to do the two-step.

"I think so."

Her mom nodded again. "Your cousin Giovanni wouldn't have been a good fit. That one, he's not ready for a nice woman. Not yet."

"I'm not sure he ever will be."

"Of course he will." Her mom turned and ran her hand

down her daughter's cheek. "When the time is right, a good man, like Angie's Devon, will come along and treasure you forever."

"I'm not looking for a man, Mama."

"I know." Her mom grinned, turned on her heel, and reached for the screen door. "But neither was Angie."

Mina did a double-take on the fiancées still dancing arm in arm. She wasn't sure she was anywhere close to ready to be treasured forever, but she sure wouldn't mind dancing.

MEET CHRIS

USA TODAY Bestselling Author of dozens of contemporary novels, including the award winning Aloha Series, Chris Keniston lives in suburban Dallas with her husband, two human children, and two canine children. Though she loves her puppies equally, she admits being especially attached to her German Shepherd rescue. After all, even dogs deserve a happily ever after.

More on Chris and all her books can be found at
www.chriskeniston.com

Follow Chris on Facebook at
ChrisKenistonAuthor

Never miss a New Release! Sign up for News from Chris:
www.chriskeniston.com/newsletter.html

Questions? Comments?
I would love to hear from you! You can reach me at:
chris@chriskeniston.com

www.ingramcontent.com/pod-product-compliance
Lightning Source LLC
Chambersburg PA
CBHW031417200726
48285CB00017BA/2410